THE FAB SIXTIES

WERE YOU THERE?

OR

DON'T YOU REMEMBER?

BY

G S WILLMOTT

WHAT'S A SPUTNIK, DAD?

CHAPTER 1

The five-year-old boy was excited. His mother, father and eleven-year-old brother had been talking about the Russian Sputnik for days and finally, the night had come. The five-year-old was me.

I remember the night well; October 9, 1957. We all walked out to the end of the driveway at 7pm. I still wasn't sure what a Sputnik was. As far as I was concerned it was just a strange name.

It was my brother who first spotted it. We looked up and saw a bright light streaming across the sky. My father tried to explain to me that this was a man-made object in space orbiting the Earth. I wasn't overly impressed. After all, Santa Claus did the same thing every Christmas.

It disappeared as quickly as it had appeared, so we all went back inside. Sputnik spotting became a nightly ritual for the next three weeks.

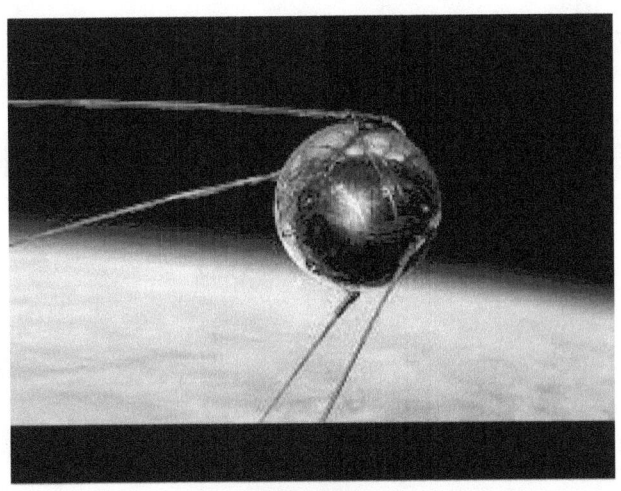

Sputnik

Los Angles 1957
The Spanish Bar & Restaurant

'What the fuck's going on? How come the Ruskies have the smarts to launch Sputnik while we, supposedly the smartest country in the world, are just sitting on our hands watching the fucking thing fly over our heads?' asked Bob.

'I don't fucking know, Bob but it's embarrassing,' said Rick.

'Well, what's Ike doing about it? He should be ramping up our program and proving to Khrushchev we have better fucking technology than those Bolshevik bastards.'

'I'm sure he's tinkering away in the White House garage as we speak.'

'It's not fucking funny, Rick. We are supposed to be the leaders of the free world.'

'We are, pal. Russia is not part of the free world.'

'You know what I mean. We are expected to be the leader in everything.'

'I'm sure we will be ahead of them in space very soon.'

Moscow October 1957

Nikita Khrushchev was in his office, which was quite austere compared to the Oval Office in the White House.

He didn't care. He had just demonstrated to the world that Russia was technologically superior to the United States by launching the first ever satellite.

The rocket used to launch Sputnik could take a nuclear warhead to anywhere in America. This fact was not lost on Dwight Eisenhower. The Russian administration led by Khrushchev was determined to lead the USA in every facet of space exploration.

Washington October 1957

Dwight Eisenhower was holding a meeting with his key cabinet members, Vice President Richard Nixon, Secretary of State, John Dulles, Secretary of Defence, Charles Wilson, and Attorney General, Herbert Brownell.

'So what? The Soviets launched a beach ball into orbit,' said Eisenhower.

'Unfortunately, the world sees it as a great accomplishment. They also see the United States as a failure as it relates to space,' said Charles Wilson.

'I've always seen satellites as strategic spying assets, not little balls beeping at the world as they go around the globe. Our satellites will spy on Russia.'

'Mr President, it won't be long before we launch our own satellite. Wernher von Braun assures me he is almost ready to launch.'

'Almost ready to come second, you mean. Look, I know everybody is trying their hardest, but we need to even up the score with the bloody Russians. We look stupid.'

Number 1 single 1957 All Shook Up – *Elvis Presley*

THE GENESIS OF THE SPACE RACE

CHAPTER 2

December 1942

Adolf Hitler knew the war was turning against him. He needed a weapon that would reverse it back in Germany's favour. He ordered the production of the V2 Rocket as a vengeance weapon intended to rain havoc on London and other strategic cities.

July 1943

Hitler and his cabinet were sitting in the Fuhrer's personal theatre. They weren't there to watch a movie. They were there to witness a film of the launching of the V2 Rocket.

'This is magnificent. At last a weapon which will eliminate the enemy without losing a man. Wernher von Braun, you are a genius. I appoint you a professor,' said Hitler.

To be promoted to the level of a professor at the age of 31 was unheard of in Germany.

Von Braun's design became the standard for all future rockets, including the Apollo series.

Hitler ordered von Braun to build 5000 rockets over the following twelve months.

To achieve this target the Germans dragged out many thousands of prisoners from the concentration camps to work in atrocious conditions. It is estimated 20,000 died constructing the V2 Rocket; many from starvation and overwork. This was by far was the highest casualty rate attributed to the V2. A total of 2724 people died in England from the explosions caused by the missiles.

Jewish Prisoners working on V2 Rocket

Jewish V2 workers on rest break

The German Resort Town of Peenemunde; site of the V2 development programme.

The V2 workforce lived under appalling conditions; there was little daylight, very little sleep, food or proper sanitation. Many were executed for attempted sabotage. Eyewitness accounts describe prisoners being hanged from cranes above the rocket assembly lines.

It has been asked whether Wernher von Braun was aware of the conditions the workforce endured in building his baby. He has always denied knowledge. Whether he did or not his design was so brilliant that it became the genesis of space flight.

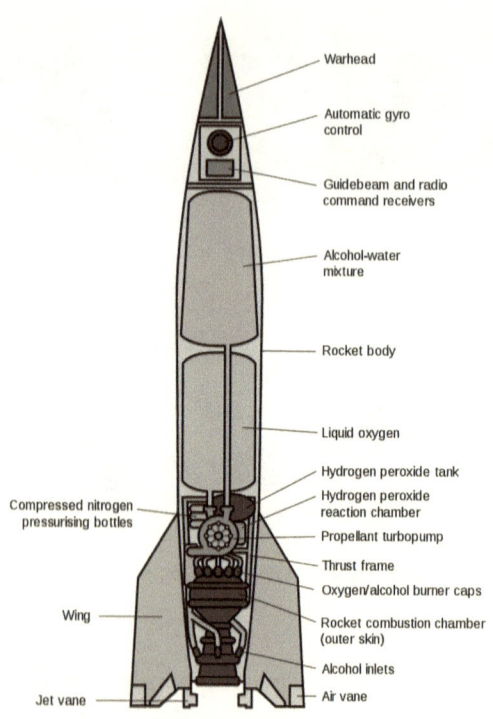

Warhead

Automatic gyro control

Guidebeam and radio command receivers

Alcohol-water mixture

Rocket body

Liquid oxygen

Hydrogen peroxide tank

Hydrogen peroxide reaction chamber

Compressed nitrogen pressurising bottles

Propellant turbopump

Thrust frame

Oxygen/alcohol burner caps

Wing

Rocket combustion chamber (outer skin)

Alcohol inlets

Jet vane

Air vane

V2 Rocket Design

Period of production	Production
Up to 15 September 1944	1900
15 September to 29 October 1944	900
29 October to 24 November 1944	600
24 November to 15 January 1945	1100
15 January to 15 February 1945	700
Total	5200

Over the first few months, approximately 3,172 V-2 rockets were fired at the following targets

Belgium 1664
The United Kingdom 1402
France 76
Netherlands 19
*Germany 11 (Remagen)

*Hitler ordered (SS) General Hans Kammler to fire 11 V2 rockets to destroy the bridge at Remagen, however, all the missiles missed their target as a consequence the Allies took control of the bridge and crossed the Rhine.

Berlin at the Conclusion of the War

The war was not going well for Germany. Most Germans now believed it was only a matter of time before capitulation.

1945

January 1-17 – Germans withdraw from the Ardennes.

January 16, 1945 – U.S. 1st and 3rd Armies link up after a month-long separation during the Battle of the Bulge.

January 17, 1945 – Soviet troops capture Warsaw, Poland.

January 26, 1945 – Soviet troops liberate Auschwitz.

February 4-11 – Roosevelt, Churchill, and Stalin meet at Yalta.

February 13/14 – Dresden is destroyed by a firestorm after Allied bombing raids.

March 6, 1945 – Last German offensive of the war begins to defend oil fields in Hungary.

March 7, 1945 – Allies take Cologne and establish a bridge across the Rhine at Remagen.

March 30, 1945 – Soviet troops capture Danzig.

In April – Allies discover stolen Nazi art and wealth hidden in German salt mines.

April 1, 1945 – U.S. troops encircle Germans in the Ruhr; Allied offensive in northern Italy.

April 12, 1945 – Allies liberate Buchenwald and Belsen concentration camps, President Roosevelt dies. Harry Truman becomes President.

April 16, 1945 – Soviet troops begin their final attack on Berlin; Americans enter Nuremberg.

April 18, 1945 – German forces in the Ruhr surrender.

April 21, 1945 – Soviets reach Berlin.

The Soviet Army was marching towards Peenemunde where the V2 rockets were manufactured. It was in the spring of 1945 that von Braun gathered his senior staff around him and asked them to decide who they should surrender to. The consensus was no to the Soviets and yes to the Americans.

SS General Kammler had been ordered by Hitler to move the V2 team to central Germany. Von Braun transported 500 of his team with forged documents to an area called Mittelwerk where they continued their work. Von Braun, fearing documents and blueprints would be destroyed by the SS, hid them in an abandoned mineshaft.

In April 1945 the Allied forces had advanced deep into Germany. Kammler ordered von Braun and his team into the Bavarian Alps under close supervision from the SS. Their orders were to execute all the engineers if it appeared the Allies would capture the V2 team.

Von Braun convinced Kammler that the engineering team would be safer from aerial bombing if they were moved to nearby villages.

Von Braun and his men escaped to Austria. On May 2, 1945, an American private on a bicycle rode past von Braun's brother who was also an engineer. He called out to him. 'My name is Magnus von Braun. My brother invented the V2 Rocket. We want to surrender.'

The US Government was delighted.

Von Braun After Surrender to the US Troops

ROCKET MAN

CHAPTER 3

The Americans knew how important von Braun and his team of engineers were to their future space program. Braun was well known to the American authorities. He topped the Black List of German scientists and engineers selected to be interrogated by military experts.

The German scientists were transferred to Munich and then onto Nordhausen and finally Witzenhausen, a town in the American zone.

Braun spent some time at Krasberg Castle where the elite of the Third Reich's economic, science and technology personnel were debriefed by U.S. and British intelligence officials.

Krasberg Castle

The program used to recruit von Braun was named Operation Paperclip.

Members of Operation Paper Clip

1945

Once the interrogation of von Braun, his brother and selected members of his team was completed, a hundred scientists were transported to America where they began work with the United States Army at Fort Bliss, Texas.

Fort Bliss Texas

Their initial task was to instruct American soldiers in launching V-2 rockets that had been captured.

Many of the German scientists and engineers became American citizens, including von Braun who took his oath in 1955.

18

Von Braun's number one priority was to convince the American Government to support the space program. Eisenhower didn't think it was particularly important; he had other priorities.

When the Soviet Union launched Sputnik, Eisenhower changed his mind and authorised the American space program.

A decision was made by the President to hand responsibility over to the Navy as they had developed the Vanguard rocket.

The world looked on as the rocket exploded on the launch pad in December 1957.

Not only had the Soviet Union launched Sputnik, but America's answer was a complete failure.

Los Angles December 1957

The Spanish Bar & Restaurant

'I'm looking forward to the launch, Bob. We may be second, but I bet your bottom dollar ours will be superior,' said Rick.

19

'Good old American ingenuity will win the day,' said Bob.

'Can I get you another bourbon, Bob? It's only ten more minutes to the launch.'

'Why not, Rick? Let's get ready to celebrate.'

Rick purchased two glasses of Wild Turkey and brought them back to the table. They had arrived early to ensure a prime spot in front of the 21-inch TV.

The countdown began. All those in the bar counted out loud in unison: 10, 9…

The flight controller announced 'lift off' the roar of the rocket engines sent chills down the spines of the patrons. The Vanguard rose slowly then fell back to earth with an enormous explosion.

'What the fuck happened there? The thing didn't get three feet off the ground!' said Bob.

Rick sighed. 'Here we go again, looking stupid to the rest of the world. The fucking Russians have launched Sputnik -1 and Sputnik - 2 and we have Flopnick - 1.'

'Yep,' Bob agreed, 'I've always been proud to be American but right now I'd rather say I was Canadian.'

Washington White House

Situation Room

Dwight Eisenhower and his key cabinet members were watching the launch with great anticipation.

Richard Nixon Vice President.

John Dulles Secretary of State

Charles Wilson Secretary of Defence

Herbert Brownell Attorney General

'Holy hell, what a disaster! This won't help our space reputation at all. The Russians are so far in front of us it's not funny. We need a win, and we need it fucking soon,' said Dwight Eisenhower.

'May I make a suggestion, Mr President?' ventured Nixon.

'What is it, Richard?'

'The Army has, as you know, its own rocket program headed up by Wernher von Braun. He's regarded as a leader in rocket science having designed the V2 Rocket for Germany. My suggestion is we hand over the project to him.'

'How soon do you think he and his team could have a rocket ready for launch?'

'I'm not sure. I will contact him immediately Mr President and get back to you shortly.'

'I look forward to hearing back from you. Does anyone else have any suggestions?'

The room remained quiet.

Richard Nixon telephoned von Braun, instructing him to come to the White House for a meeting.

The space engineer had a good idea of why he had been summoned.

The meeting had been arranged for Tuesday 29 December.

White House

Wernher von Braun flew into Washington from Texas. He caught a cab to the White House where he was due to meet with Vice President Richard Nixon.

He waited in the Vice President's anteroom for fifteen minutes, quite a short period of time by Nixon's standards.

'The Vice President will see you now,' announced the receptionist.

Von Braun entered the opulent office.

'Mr von Braun it's a pleasure to meet you.'

'It's an honour to meet you, Mr Vice President.'

21

'Please call me Richard.'

'Please call me Wernher.'

'Can I arrange to get you a coffee or perhaps tea?'

'A coffee would be most welcome, Richard.'

Nixon ordered the coffee over the intercom.

'Now, while we wait for our coffee, I take it you viewed the disastrous aborted launch of Vanguard?'

'I'm afraid the whole world did, Richard.'

'Yes, I'm afraid you are right. We need to make up a lot of ground. The Russians are way ahead of us.'

'I agree the way they are going it won't be long before they launch a man into orbit.'

'Yes, and we are having trouble launching a basketball. I believe you and your team are developing an alternative rocket?'

'I'm not sure we view it as an alternative rocket, Richard, but yes we are well on the way to completing what we call the Redstone Rocket.'

'How long before you think it would be ready for launch?'

'Both my team and the Army strongly believe we could launch a satellite next January.'

'My God that's next month.'

'That's right, but we would need authorisation immediately.'

'Please wait here, Wernher. I'll see if I can see the President.'

Von Braun had to wait only twenty minutes before Nixon returned.

'The President has authorised the project to begin immediately. I suggest you fly back to Fort Bliss as soon as a flight is available.'

'Thank you, Richard, I can assure you that you and the President won't be disappointed.'

'I sincerely hope not Wernher.'

SUCCESS

AT LAST

CHAPTER 4

Wernher von Braun returned to Fort Bliss with an authorised budget from the President to complete constructing the Redstone Rocket. He gathered his team together and informed them of their mandate. The team of engineers and scientists worked around the clock to achieve the January deadline.

The Redstone was on the launch pad ready to launch on January 31, 1958.

Los Angles January 31, 1958

The Spanish Bar & Restaurant

'Here we go again, Bob. I'm not really sure if I want to see this.'
'Come on, Rick; have faith, my son. They couldn't fuck it up again.'
'Yes, they could.'
'Okay, they've started the count down.'
The flight controller began the count. When he reached 2, the atmosphere in the bar was electric and more than one patron had their fingers crossed.

0; we have lift off

Redstone Rocket Launch

The rocket's powerful engines lifted the rocket skywards until she reached orbit. Everybody in the bar cheered and hugged. Bob and Rick couldn't let one another go.

'We did it! We fucking did it.'

Top single 1958; Poor Little Fool, *Ricky Nelson*

White House Situation Room

Dwight Eisenhower and his key cabinet members were watching once again with great trepidation.

Vice President, Richard Nixon.

Secretary of State, John Dulles

Secretary of Defence, Charles Wilson

Attorney General, Herbert Brownell

The atmosphere in the situation room was palpable. At last, they had joined the space race, albeit well behind the Russians.

'Okay, we not only need to catch the Russians, but we also need to beat the bastards,' said Charles Wilson.

'I agree. We can't rest on our laurels this is just one small step,' said President Eisenhower.

Two months after the successful launch of Explorer, the Americans launched the first solar-powered satellite. Two months later, they launched the first communications satellite.

The space race had begun in earnest.

In January 1959 the Soviet Union launched its Luna satellite, which flew close to the moon.

'Fucking hell the Russians got close to the moon. My God, they could almost piss in one of its craters. What have we got up our sleeve to make them nervous?' asked the President.

'Sir, we are launching a weather satellite on February 17, and we will be the first to put a satellite into a polar orbit on February 28,' said John Dulles.

'Well that's just dandy. The Russians are the first in space, the first to launch a live animal and first to get close to the moon and we're the first to launch a fucking weather satellite to tell us when it will snow rather than looking out the window.'

'The most exciting news we have, Mr President, is our intention to launch a spy satellite with a powerful camera. The Russians won't get away with anything without us knowing about it,' said Charles Wilson.

'Now that is good news, Charley. When will it be launched?'

'June 25th, sir.'

LET THE RACE BEGIN

CHAPTER 5

June 25, 1959

Discoverer was the name given to the spy satellite. It was launched successfully, but failed to reach orbit, rendering it useless. Eisenhower was devastated as he always thought satellites were only useful for spying on the Russians.

August 7, 1959

The USA took the first photograph of Earth from space.

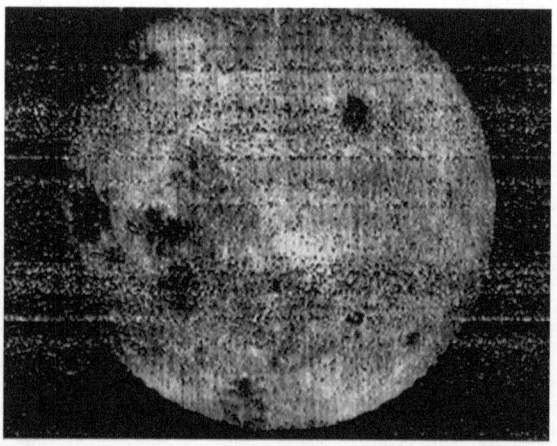

For a short time, the Americans thought they were making progress in the space race. Their belief was, despite the Soviet Union having bigger rockets, the USA had better more accurate guidance systems.

September 14, 1959

When the Soviets crashed Luna 2 onto the moon all thoughts of superiority diminished.

'Well, here we go again! We think we're making some headway and the bastards land a satellite on the moon,' said the president.

'They didn't actually land on the moon, sir; they crashed into it,' said Richard Nixon.

'I don't care how you word it, Richard; they have a Russian satellite on the bloody moon. The closest we've got to it is 37,000 miles.'

October 7, 1959

The Soviets published happy snaps of the dark side of the moon. The Americans hadn't even thought it possible.

Top single, The Battle of New Orleans, *Johnny Horton*

July 5, 1960

At last President Eisenhower and his administration received good news when the second spy satellite was launched successfully into orbit and began sending images of Russian military sites.

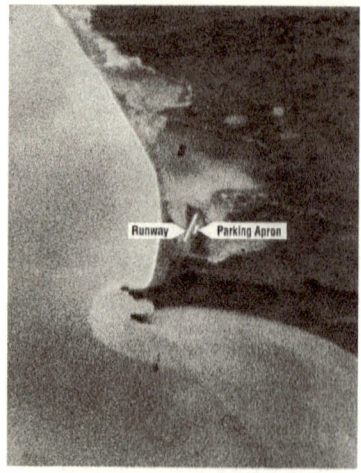

Soviet Air Field

August 19, 1960

President Khrushchev decided he should meet Belka and Strelka before they undertook their journey into space. Both dogs were brought to his office their handlers conducted the introductions. After the president patted both dogs they were led out of his office and taken back to the space centre.

The two canine space travellers were the first animals to orbit the Earth and return safely.

Belka and Strelka ready to blast off

The Americans were not to be outdone; they found a hominid to volunteer for a space mission.

Ham the Astrochimp,

Ham was launched from Cape Canaveral on a flight that lasted sixteen minutes and thirty-nine seconds. The only injury sustained was a bruised nose.

There's a New President in Town

Chapter 6

1960 was an eventful year. America's first Catholic president was elected. John Fitzgerald Kennedy, commonly known as JFK, won a close election against Richard Nixon. He was 43 when elected; only one year older than Theodore Roosevelt, the youngest president in US history.

Kennedy was concerned that the Russians were winning the space race. He spoke to his most trusted advisers to determine a strategy.

However, he was preoccupied with a plan presented to him by the CIA, which would dispose of Fidel Castro in Cuba. The space race could wait a while.

Top single 1960— Theme from a Summer Place, *Percy Faith*

I have a Cunning Plan

Allen Dulles, the CIA Director was sitting in his office at CIA headquarters in Langley, Virginia.

The time was 9am and he was due to meet with President Eisenhower in the Oval Office at 9.30am.

He picked up his internal phone.

> 'Sharon has my car arrived yet?'
> 'Yes sir, shall I tell the driver you are on your way?'
> 'Yes, thank you, I'm going down to the car park now.'

Dulles caught the secure lift down four floors, accompanied by two CIA operatives.

There were three limousines. He entered the middle vehicle and the other two were occupied by members of his security team.

The drive took ten minutes and then he was ushered into the president's anteroom.

He waited twenty minutes before being invited in by a CIA agent, one of 1200 who provided security for the president and his staff.

'Good morning, Mr President.'

'Good morning, Allen— please take a seat. Can I order you a coffee?'

'Yes thank you, white with one sugar.'

'I should know by now.'

'Mr President, I asked to see you for a very good reason. As you know, Cuba has become very aggressive towards the United States. We at the CIA believe that they have become a puppet state of the USSR. We also believe Cuba poses a real danger to our security.'

'What are you proposing, Allen? If we invade Cuba we then invite the Soviets to declare war on the United States.'

'Mr President, my department has devised a plan for your approval. Firstly, we need to replace the Castro regime with a more tolerant leader who would become an ally of the United States. We need to achieve this without the perception of any U.S. intervention.'

'That's all very grand, Allen, but how are we going to achieve this?'

'The first stage would be to initiate a powerful propaganda campaign against the Castro regime. The second stage will be to build a powerful intelligence network within Cuba. The third and final stage would be to create an invasion force of exiled Cubans to invade the island. Our support would be clandestine but intense.'

'We can't be involved in an invasion directly. Is that what you are proposing?'

'No sir, we are not proposing direct intervention. Our suggested plan is to mass a Cuban exile army to invade. The USA would clandestinely fund the invasion force and provide all the necessary weapons and equipment.'

'I'll support the plan in principle. Begin your preparations. I'll wait before I give my final sign off.'

'Yes, sir. No doubt you would like to be kept informed.'

'I would, but don't commit anything on paper. Face to face should be the only communication.'

'Of course, sir.'

The director left the Oval Office, well pleased with the meeting.

When Dulles returned to Langley he summoned Deputy Director Richard Bissell Jr.

'Dick, I have just briefed Eisenhower on our proposed action re Cuba. He has approved us to develop a plan for the invasion.'

'That's excellent, Allen; I'll get started straight away.'

'Who do you have in mind for your team?'

'Initially David Phillips, Gerry Droller and Howard Hunt. They are all very experienced operatives and were instrumental in the Guatemalan coup.'

The 1954 Guatemalan coup was codenamed Operation PBSUCCESS. It was a cover operation carried out by the CIA. The democratically elected President Jacob Arbenz was overthrown. The U.S. installed Carlos Castillo Armas, a military dictator who was pro USA.

Dulles instructed Gerry Droller to attend a meeting in the Director's Office.

'Good afternoon, Gerry; take a seat. The Director has informed me that we have approval to begin preparations for Operation Bay of Pigs.'

'That's great, sir; where do you want me to start?'

'I want you to go down to Florida and recruit Cuban exiles who would be willing to take part in an invasion force. You can tell them we will train them and provide all the necessary weaponry and equipment, including boats.'

'Yes sir. How many are we looking to recruit?'

'Ideally 2000, but 1500 would suffice.'

'I take it you want me to leave immediately?'

'I do.'

Droller made arrangements to move to Florida. Raising a dissident force of this size would not be achieved overnight.

Droller's first point of contact was with ex Castro supporter Manuel Francisco Artime Buesa. Manuel had fought alongside Castro and Che Guevara in the Cuban revolution. He became discontented with the regime and, with the help of the CIA, fled to Miami.

The CIA gave the exile army the name of Brigade 2506.

July 1960

The CIA Director was called to a meeting with President Eisenhower in the Oval Office at the White House.

'Allen, thanks for coming— I appreciate it.'

'With respect, Mr President, when you summon me I come.'

'I think we need to brief Senator Kennedy on our plans for Cuba. All indications are he'll be the next president. If he is, this operation will take place under his watch.'

'Yes, I fully agree, sir. We don't want any last-minute hitches.'

CIA Director Dulles arranged to meet the Senator at the Kennedy home at Hyannis Port on Cape Cod.

Kennedy Beach House

July 23, 1960

'Welcome to my humble abode, Allen; can I offer you a drink?'

'Thank you, Senator— maybe after I brief you on the Cuban situation.'

'As you wish. What can you tell me about your plans to get rid of that man Castro?'

The CIA Director gave Senator Kennedy a full briefing, including the training of Cuban exiles and the proposed invasion. The briefing lasted over two hours.

'Thank you, Allen; that was most informative. In principle I support the operation. Please keep me informed of your progress. Now, can I offer you a malt whisky? It's Macallan, my favourite.'

'Thank you, John. I would love one.'

September 19, 1960

CIA Director Allen Dulles briefs John F Kennedy in his Washington office.

Soon after Senator Kennedy attacks the Eisenhower administration for "permitting a communist menace to arise only ninety miles from the shores of the United States".

Richard Nixon running against Kennedy denounces the Democrat's position on Cuba. He too has been briefed on the CIA's plans.

November 1960

White House

CIA Director Dulles and Deputy Director Bissell were summoned to meet with President Eisenhower to brief the President.

'How are we progressing in establishing a Cuban government in exile? As far as I see it that is a critical part of the plan.'

'We are making real progress. We are both confident it will be in place by the time the exiles hit the beaches.'

'I'm going along with you boys, but I want to be sure the damn thing works.'

'It will work, sir, I can assure you.'

November 18, 1960

Dulles and Bissell visited President-Elect John Kennedy at the family's Palm Beach summer home to brief him on the Bay of Pigs operation.

December 6, 1960

President Eisenhower met with the President-Elect to brief him on the Cuban operation.

January 19, 1961

Washington

President Eisenhower invited President-Elect Kennedy to a meeting in the Oval Office.

'Welcome to your new home, Jack. How does it feel?'
'It's not mine yet, Dwight.'
'It will be in a week or so.'
'Did you invite me here to admire the office or was there something else you wish to discuss?'

'This will be your final briefing from me re the Cuban operation. It will be your responsibility from now on. What I need to know is will you endorse it? If not, I will wind it up immediately.'

'I support it, Dwight, although I'm concerned the United States could be publicly involved. Would you endorse American support even if we were exposed to a greater military involvement?'

'Yes, I would. We cannot tolerate Castro and his communist regime to continue.'

'Well, you'd better wish me luck. It's not how I envisaged my first few months in office.'

January 22, 1961

Several members of the incoming Kennedy Administration including Dean Rusk, Robert McNamara, Chester Bowles, and Robert Kennedy, receive a briefing on the Cuba operation at the State Department

January 28, 1961

Kennedy receives his first official briefing as President on the Cuban operation in a meeting attended by Vice President Lyndon B. Johnson, Secretary of State Dean Rusk, Defence Secretary Robert McNamara, National Security Adviser McGeorge Bundy, CIA Director Dulles, General Lemnitzer, Chairman of the Joint Chiefs of Staff, Assistant Secretaries Mann and Nitze, and Tracy Barnes of the CIA.

April 17, 1961

Over 1400 armed Cuban exiles landed at the Bay of Pigs in Cuba in the United States-supported effort to spark the overthrow of Fidel Castro's regime. The invasion was an infamous disaster: the Cuban government, forewarned, defended with a force of more than 20,000, then 1202 of the exiles were captured and 114 killed in action.

The Bay of Pigs was an embarrassment for the newly elected President, as it was he who approved the plan, signing off on its implementation.

Bay of Pigs Invasion

On 21 December 1962, Cuban Prime Minister Fidel Castro and James B. Donovan, a US lawyer aided by Milan C. Miskovsky, a CIA legal officer, signed an agreement to exchange 1,113 prisoners for US$53 million in food and medicine, sourced from private donations and from companies expecting tax concessions. On 24 December 1962, some prisoners were flown to Miami. Others followed on the ship *African Pilot*, plus about 1,000 family members were also allowed to leave Cuba. On 29th of December, 1962, President Kennedy and his wife Jacqueline attended a "welcome back" ceremony for Brigade 2506 veterans at the Orange Bowl in Miami, Florida.

Kennedy knew he needed to divert attention away from the Cuban disaster. He also knew he needed to demonstrate America's space superiority.

'Lyndon, I've asked you to come to the Oval Office in your capacity of chairman of the National Aeronautics and Space Council,' said President Kennedy.

'How may I help. Mr President?'

'I want you to investigate whether the United States could be first in putting a laboratory into space or orbiting a man around the moon or better still landing a man on the moon. I need to know if it could be done and how much such a project would cost.'

'I'll do my best, Mr President. I agree we need something outstanding to beat the Russians,' said Lyndon B Johnson.

Johnson arranged a meeting with the newly appointed administrator of NASA, James E Webb, who advised the best option was putting a man on the moon.

'James, can you determine an approximation of the budget required and report back to me please?'

'Yes, Mr Vice President, but it could take a few weeks.'

In time, the Vice President received a phone call from James Webb.

'Hello, Mr Vice President I was wondering if you could see me to discuss the budget for the moon landing.'

'Yes, certainly; you can come this afternoon if that's convenient.'

'Okay, what time?'

'Why don't we make it five?'

'I'll see you then.'

Webb arrived just before five and waited in the anteroom. He didn't have to wait long.

'Come in James and take a seat. Can I offer you a whisky? The sun is well and truly over the yardarm.'

'Yes, thank you Mr Vice President, that would be most welcome.'

'You can call me LBJ, James; no need for formalities when we are alone.'

LBJ poured two generous whiskies and handed one to Webb.

'Right what have you got for me, James?'

'We estimate the Government would need to allocate $22 billion.'

'Goodness me, that's a lot of money.'

'We have a long way to go when you consider we only just launched a chimp.'

'When you put it that way, I suppose you're right. Let me discuss it with the President.

Lyndon Johnson arranged to see President Kennedy to discuss the moon landing and the associated cost.

He was pleasantly surprised when President Kennedy accepted the budget and approved the project. An American would be walking on the moon inside ten years.

Johnson arranged meetings with Wernher von Braun and some captains of industry, all of whom were enthusiastic.

May 25, 1961

President Kennedy stood before Congress and proposed that the United States "should commit itself to achieve the goal, before this decade is out, of landing a man on the moon and returning him safely to Earth."

Top single 1961

Tossin' and Turnin' Bobby Lewis

September 12, 1962

Rice University Stadium, Utah.

President Kennedy announced his grand plan to 40,000 people in the stadium and 3 billion around the globe.

We set sail on this new sea because there is new knowledge to be gained, and new rights to be won, and they must be won and used for the progress of all people. For space science, like nuclear science and all technology, has no conscience of its own. Whether it will become a force for good or ill depends on man, and only if the United States occupies a position of pre-eminence can we help decide whether this new ocean will be a sea of peace or a new terrifying theatre of war. I do not say that we should or will go unprotected against the hostile misuse of space any more than we go unprotected against the hostile use of land or sea, but I do say that space can be explored and mastered without feeding the fires of war, without repeating the mistakes that man has made in extending his writ around this globe of ours.

There is no strife, no prejudice, and no national conflict in outer space as yet. Its hazards are hostile to us all. Its conquest deserves the best of all mankind, and its opportunity for peaceful cooperation may never come again. But why, some say, the Moon? Why choose this as our goal? And they may well ask, why climb the highest mountain? Why, 35 years ago, fly the Atlantic? Why does Rice play Texas?

We choose to go to the Moon! *We choose to go to the Moon...We choose to go to the Moon in this decade and do the other things, not because they are easy, but because they are hard; because that goal will serve to organize and measure the best of our energies and skills, because that challenge is one that we are willing to accept, one we are unwilling to postpone, and one we intend to win, and the others, too.*

THE COLD WAR

CHAPTER 7

August 12-13, 1961

Berlin Wall

East German soldiers sealed the border between East Berlin and West Berlin with barbed wire. Soon after, East German authorities began to build a concrete and brick wall to close off the two sectors permanently. It stood as a beacon to the Cold War for the next 28 years.

Winston Churchill said, "From Stettin in the Baltic to Trieste in the Adriatic, an iron curtain has descended across the continent."

At the end of World War II the defeated Germany was divided into four Allied occupation zones. This also applied to Berlin, the former capital of the Third Reich. Although the city was well inside the Soviet zone it too was divided into four zones. The USA, Britain and France decided to unite their zones into a single autonomous entity – the Federal Republic of Germany (West Germany).

The Soviets were furious, and they created a land blockade of West Berlin, endeavouring to coerce the west to evacuate the city.

The West overcame the blockade, implementing an enormous airlift mainly by the USA and Britain to supply food and fuel and other essential supplies.

Knowing they had been defeated, the USSR ended the blockade in May 1949.

Berlin Airlift

Tensions between East and West were intensifying. The East was unhappy about losing their skilled labour and intellectuals to the West.

Between 1949 and 1961, 2.5 million East Germans escaped from East to West Germany. By August 1961 approximately 2000 East Germans were crossing into the West every day. This loss was having a devastating effect on the East German economy. Something had to be done. Nikita Khrushchev ordered access between East and West Berlin be closed.

On a hot night in August, hundreds of East German soldiers laid barbed wire, sixty miles in total, creating a barrier between East and West Berlin.

East Berliners woke on the 13th of August to discover they had been imprisoned. The number of checkpoints had been reduced dramatically, making it difficult to cross over for legitimate business.

A six-foot-high, 96-mile-long wall of concrete blocks, complete with guard towers, machine gun posts and searchlights, soon replaced the wire. East German officers known as Volkspolizei ("Volpos") patrolled the Berlin Wall, day and night.

Constructing the Berlin Wall

The Berlin Wall became an iconic symbol of the Cold War. President Kennedy gave his famous speech "Ich bin ein Berliner" standing in front of the wall.

In 1970 the height of the wall was raised to 10 feet to lessen the number of escapes. Between 1961 and 1989 when the wall came down, over 5000 East Germans escaped. Tragically 239 died attempting to cross over.

One of many Memorials along the wall

The Train to Freedom

August 13, 1961

Harry Deterling, his wife Ingrid and four boys lived in a quiet neighbourhood in Berlin. At war's end, Harry discovered he was now an East Berliner. He and his family were effectively under communist Soviet control. His brother and sister lived in West Berlin. Harry and his family made regular visits to see his siblings, but that all changed on 13 August 1961.

Friedrich, the eldest boy, woke early and decided to go for a bike ride. What he saw astonished him and he rode back to his house as quickly as he could.

He knocked on his parents' bedroom door.

> 'Mama, Papa wake up! I must tell you something very important.'
> 'Friedrich, what time is it?'
> 'It's six o'clock. I know it's early but something terrible has happened.'
> 'Are you hurt?'
> 'No, but you must come and look.'
> 'Okay, give us time to dress. Put the kettle on.'

Harry, being a train driver, was used to getting up early but Ingrid was not. She decided to stay in bed and let Harry see whatever Friedrich was carrying on about.

Harry entered the kitchen hoping for a cup of coffee, but none was made.

> 'Papa come and see, then you can have your coffee.'

Father and son walked out onto the street. At the far end, Harry could see floodlights and large rolls of barbed wire being rolled out to form an eight-foot fence.

'Why are they doing this, Papa?'

'To keep us in.'

'Why?'

'Because they are scared we'll all leave East Berlin and go to live in West Berlin.'

'But I don't want to leave our home, Papa.'

'I know you don't, son. Come on, we'd better go home. You promised me a coffee.'

By the time Harry and Friedrich arrived back, Ingrid and the other three boys were sitting around the kitchen table.

'So, what was so urgent?'

'I'll tell you later.'

From that day on Harry began plotting his and his family's escape.

Harry noticed there was a disused train track leading from the eastern side of the wall into the west. All he had to do was steer a train through the barbed wire fence and into freedom.

Harry chose December 5, his 38th birthday, to execute his and his family's escape. His coal stoker was in on the plan and was a willing participant.

Under cover of Christmas drinks, the Deterlings invited their family and close friends to their house. They invited all their guests to join them. All but a few agreed to go. Harry was concerned that his adventurous plan would get back to the East German authorities. You never knew who you could trust.

Deterling persuaded his bosses to allow him to run an extra locomotive to give him more experience. They agreed.

Those who agreed to take part in the daring escape were instructed to meet at the railway yard at 7.30pm.

Harry began his journey to freedom. Harmut Lichy, the coal stoker, shovelled in the coal at a frenetic pace.

There were a few unsuspecting passengers who knew nothing of the plan. Most stayed in West Berlin, but a few returned to the East. All in all there were 32 people on board.

8.50pm

The locomotive passed through the last stop in East Berlin, Albrechtshof Station, without slowing down. The border guards were taken completely unawares.

Now the train was heading straight for the East West border crossing. Deterling opened up the throttle and he also disconnected the emergency brake so the locomotive could not be stopped.

The passengers all lay on the carriage floor. Deterling climbed into the coal car with Lichv the stoker. They had no idea whether the border guards would open fire.

The train smashed through the fence at 50 miles per hour and entered West Berlin.

The West German police arrived and escorted the passengers into a safe zone.

East German guards tear up the railway line

The following day the East Germans tore up the track.

This was one of many audacious escapes from East to West.

There were other amazing escapes demonstrating bravery and the will to live in a free democratic environment.

Wolfgang Engels joined the East German Army in 1959. In the beginning, the work was enjoyable but as time went on he became discontented. His time was spent arresting dissidents and guarding the checkpoints along the barbed wire fence. He saw more than one East Berliner shot dead trying to escape.

He helped build the Berlin Wall in 1961 and two years later he made the decision to escape the repressive regime.

April 16, 1963

Wolfgang stole a tank from his barracks and drove it to the wall. He smashed into the concrete barrier at full speed. The tank did do some damage but not enough to drive the tank through. Engels climbed out of the tank and began to scale the wall but got caught up in the barbed wire. Two East German guards, both known to Wolfgang, opened fire, wounding him twice.

Some West Berliners heard the ruckus and the shots from the pub where they were drinking. They managed to extricate the wounded Engels from the wire and carried him into the pub and laid him down on the counter. He was unconscious, but a doctor in the house revived him. He opened his eyes, turned his head and looked at the liquor on the shelves. He saw Jim Beam Bourbon, McCallum Scotch and various other western brands.

'Thank God I made it.'

It was love that prompted Heinz Meixner's daring scheme. While working in East Berlin, the Austrian fell for Margarete Thurau, but authorities denied her permission to marry him back in his home country. Meixner decided to get her and his future mother-in-law out on his own terms. He hired an Austin Healy convertible, removed the windshield and let a little air out of the tyres to bring the vehicle even lower to the ground. On May 5, 1963, with Thurau and her mother hiding in the back, Meixner drove the car to the border post dubbed Checkpoint Charlie. When Meixner reached the inspection point, he ducked his head and accelerated, driving under the barrier into West Berlin.

Aircraft mechanic Hans Peter Strelczyk got his inspiration for his escape from an East German TV program on the history of ballooning. Together with his friend Gunter Wetzel, he made a hot air balloon to carry both families into the west. The friends built the engine from propane cylinders and their wives stitched together bed sheets for the balloon. After a failed first attempt, the two families finally soared over the Wall on September 16, 1979, landing after 30 minutes in a blackberry bush on West German soil.

November 9, 1989

Tear down this wall!

Masses of East and West Germans alike gathered at the Berlin Wall and began to climb over and dismantle it. As this symbol of Cold War repression was destroyed, East and West Germany became one nation again, signing a formal treaty of unification on October 3, 1990.

"Tear Down This Wall" Ronald Regan Friday, June 12, 1987

CIGARS AND NUKES

CHAPTER 8

Cuban Missile Crisis October 1962

Robert McNamara

October 15, 1962

Robert McNamara was sitting at his desk going over some intelligence papers relating to the conflict in Vietnam.

He was concerned the Viet Cong insurgency had expanded in South Vietnam. McNamara had authorised U.S. military personnel to fly combat missions and to accompany South Vietnamese soldiers in ground operations to find and defeat the insurgents. Secrecy was the official U.S. policy concerning the extent of U.S. military involvement in South Vietnam. McNamara kept the information very close to his chest. Colonel Biggs, attached to intelligence, requested a meeting with the Secretary of Defence. He stated it was extremely important. He was granted a meeting at 10am on 15 October at the Pentagon.

Colonel Biggs was extremely nervous, for he had never met the Secretary before, let alone briefed him.
He waited in the anteroom for over half an hour, by which time he had developed beads of sweat on his forehead and his hands were clammy. Finally, he was beckoned into the large, beautifully decorated office.

'Good morning, Colonel Biggs! Please take a seat. Can I arrange to get you a coffee?'

'Thank you sir; white with no sugar, please.'

'It shouldn't be long.'

'In the meantime maybe you could enlighten me on the purpose of your visit.'

'Sir, as you are aware the United States takes regular reconnaissance photos of Cuba from our U2 spy plane?'

'Yes, naturally I'm aware of that. Have we found something interesting?'

'Yes, sir, we have. May I show you the photos that are causing concern?'

MEDIUM RANGE BALLISTIC MISSILE BASE IN CUBA

SAN CRISTOBAL

LAUNCH POSITION

MISSILE-READY TENTS

MISSILE ERECTORS

MISSILE TRANSPORTERS

12 PROB GUIDELINE MISSILES

HEAVY EQUIPMENT

5 MISSILE DOLLIES

20' LONG CYLINDRICAL TANKS

MISSILE TRANSPORTERS

'We are convinced the USSR is building nuclear missile launch pads in Cuba which will pose a direct threat to the United States.'

'Holy hell, I need to call the President immediately.'

McNamara contacted the White House. President Kennedy was occupied in a meeting with his brother, Bobby Kennedy.

McNamara informed the President's assistant he needed to speak to the President urgently.

When the Secretary of Defence says it's urgent you listen.

'Mr President, I have received some very disturbing information in relation to Cuba. May I see you as soon as it's convenient?'

'Come on over, Rob. I've got Bobby with me. I'll ask him to stay for your briefing.'

McNamara arrived at the White House twenty-five minutes later, armed with the reconnaissance photos.

He only had to wait five minutes before being invited into the Oval Office.

'Mr President, we have received irrefutable evidence that the Soviets are close to completing missile bases which will accommodate Soviet SS-4 medium-range ballistic missiles aimed at the United States.'

'What evidence do you have?'

'Photographs from a U2 plane flying over Cuba yesterday.'

'Show me,' said the President in an agitated voice. 'Fucking Russians, I don't believe it. We need to convene the Executive Committee to determine our response.'

Executive Committee

President John F. Kennedy meets with members of the Executive Committee of the National Security Council (EXCOMM) regarding the crisis in Cuba. Clockwise from top right side of table: Under Secretary of State George Ball, Secretary of State Dean Rusk, President Kennedy, Secretary of Defence Robert S. McNamara, Deputy Secretary of Defence Roswell Gilpatric, Chairman of the Joint Chiefs of Staff General Maxwell D. Taylor, Assistant Secretary of Defence for International Security Affairs Paul Nitze, Acting Director of the United States Information Agency (USIA) Donald Wilson, Special Counsel to the President Theodore C. Sorensen, Special Assistant to the President for National Security McGeorge Bundy (mostly hidden), Secretary of the Treasury C. Douglas Dillon, Vice President Lyndon B. Johnson (mostly hidden), Attorney General Robert F. Kennedy, former U.S. Ambassador to the Soviet Union Llewellyn Thompson, Director of the Arms Control and Disarmament Agency (ACDA) William C. Foster, and Director of the Central Intelligence Agency (CIA) John McCone (mostly hidden behind Director Foster). Cabinet Room, White House, Washington, D.C.

Tuesday 16, October

The most dangerous thirteen days in the world's history has begun. The Executive Committee is briefed on the U2 discoveries in Cuba. The most dominant advice to President Kennedy comes from Dean Rusk, Secretary of State and Robert McNamara, Defence Secretary.

'One course of action is to bomb the missile bases and follow up with an invasion,' advises Dean Rusk.

'Another alternative is to implement a naval quarantine with the threat of additional military action if required,' says McNamara.

The second alternative is the one favoured by President Kennedy.

JFK maintains his normal presidential schedule so as not to alarm the American people.

The Executive Committee continues to meet to discuss the crisis.

Wednesday, October 17

McNamara orders military units to the south-eastern area of the country, having viewed more intelligence photos from an additional U-2 flight over Cuba showing additional sites and 32 missiles. President Kennedy is briefed but continues his schedule as he attends a church service at St Mathew's Cathedral in observance of the National Day of Prayer. He has lunch with Crown Prince Hasan of Libya, and then travels to Connecticut to support Democratic congressional candidates.

October 18

JFK and Andrei Gromyko Meet

President Kennedy receives the Soviet Foreign Minister Andrei Gromyko in the Oval Office.

The Russian assures President Kennedy that any Soviet aid to Cuba is purely defensive and does not represent a threat to the United States.

Kennedy does not reveal his knowledge of the offensive missiles, but he reads to Gromyko his public warning delivered on September 4 that the "gravest consequences" would follow if significant Soviet offensive weapons were introduced into Cuba.

October 19

President Kennedy leaves for a scheduled campaign trip to Ohio and Illinois. In Washington, his advisers continue the debate over the necessary and appropriate course of action.

October 20

President Kennedy returns suddenly to Washington. After five hours of discussion with top advisers, including McNamara and Dean Rusk, he decides on the quarantine option. Plans for deploying naval units are drawn up and work is begun on a speech to notify the American people of the crisis.

October 21

After attending Mass at St. Stephen's Church with Mrs Kennedy, the President meets with General Walter Sweeney of the Tactical Air Command. He is informed that an air strike could not guarantee 100% destruction of the missiles.

President Kennedy's Diary

October 22

President Kennedy phones former Presidents Hoover, Truman and Eisenhower to brief them of the situation. Meetings to coordinate all actions continue. Kennedy formally establishes the Executive Committee of the National Security Council and instructs it to meet daily during the crisis. Kennedy briefs the cabinet and congressional leaders on the situation. Kennedy also informs British Prime Minister Harold Macmillan of the situation by telephone.

President Kennedy writes to Nikita Khrushchev, Premier of the Soviet Union, prior to addressing the American public on live television.

THE WHITE HOUSE

WASHINGTON

October 22, 1962

Sir:

A copy of the statement I am making tonight concerning developments in Cuba and the reaction of my Government thereto has been handed to your Ambassador in Washington. In view of the gravity of the developments to which I refer, I want you to know immediately and accurately the position of my Government in this matter.

In our discussions and exchanges on Berlin and other international questions, the one thing that has most concerned me has been the possibility that your Government would not correctly understand the will and determination of the United States in any given situation, since I have not assumed that you or any other sane man would, in this nuclear age, deliberately plunge the world into war which it is crystal clear no country could win and which could only result in catastrophic consequences to the whole world, including the aggressor.

At our meeting in Vienna and subsequently, I expressed our readiness and desire to find, through peaceful negotiation, a solution to any and all problems that divide us. At the same time, I made clear that in view of the objectives of the ideology to which you adhere, the United States could not tolerate any action on your part which in a major way disturbed the existing over-all balance of power in the world. I stated that an attempt to force abandonment of our responsibilities and commitments in Berlin would constitute such an action and that the United States would resist with all the power at its command.

It was in order to avoid any incorrect assessment on the part of your Government with respect to Cuba that I publicly stated that if certain developments in Cuba took place, the United States would do whatever must be done to protect its own security and that of its allies.

Moreover, the Congress adopted a resolution expressing its support of this declared policy. Despite this, the rapid development of long-range missile bases and other offensive weapons systems in Cuba has proceeded. I must tell you that the United States is determined that this threat to the security of this hemisphere be removed. At the same time, I wish to point out that the action we are taking is the minimum necessary to remove the threat to the security of the nations of this hemisphere. The fact of this minimum response should not be taken as a basis, however, for any misjudgement on your part.

I hope that your Government will refrain from any action which would widen or deepen this already grave crisis and that we can agree to resume the path of peaceful negotiation.

Sincerely,

His Excellency
Nikita S. Khrushchev
Chairman of the Council of Ministers
of the Union of Soviet Socialist Republics
MOSCOW

At 7:00 p.m. Kennedy speaks on television, revealing the evidence of Soviet missiles in Cuba and calling for their removal. He also announces the establishment of a naval quarantine around the island until the Soviet Union agrees to dismantle the missile sites and to make certain that no additional missiles will be shipped to Cuba. Approximately one hour before the speech, Secretary of State Dean Rusk formally notifies Soviet Ambassador Anatoly Dobrynin of the contents of the President's speech.

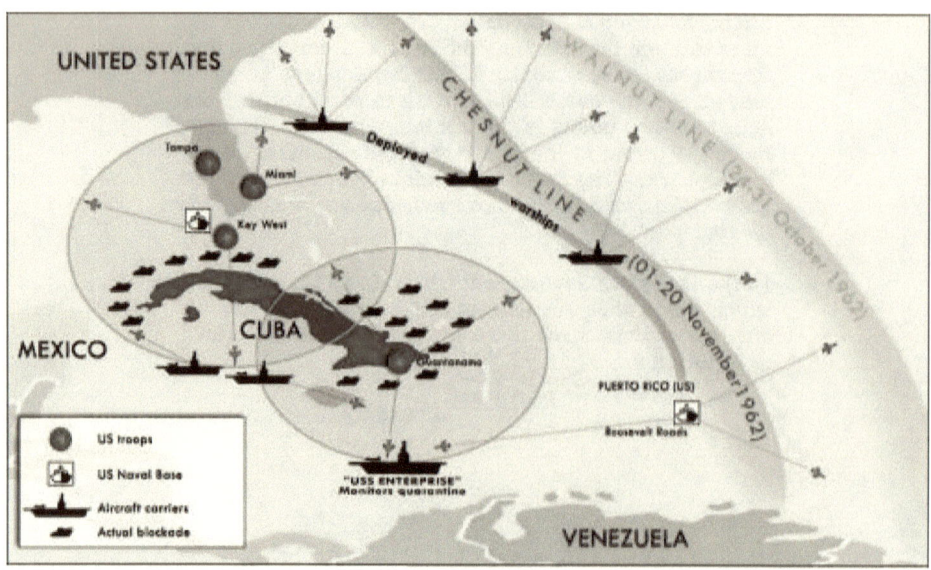

October 23

Assistant Secretary of State for Inter-American Affairs Edwin Martin seeks a resolution of support from the Organization of American States. Ambassador to the United Nations, Adlai Stevenson, lays the matter before the U.N. Security Council. The ships of the naval quarantine fleet move into place around Cuba. Soviet submarines threaten the quarantine by moving into the Caribbean area. Soviet freighters bound for Cuba with military supplies stop dead in the water, but the oil tanker Bucharest continues towards Cuba. In the evening Robert Kennedy meets with Ambassador Dobrynin at the Soviet Embassy.
The President receives a letter from the Russian President.

After the Organization of American States endorses the quarantine, President Kennedy asks Khrushchev to halt any Russian ships that are heading towards Cuba. The President's greatest concern is that a US Navy vessel will be forced to fire upon a Russian vessel, possibly igniting a war between the superpowers.

October 24

Chairman Khrushchev replies indignantly to President Kennedy's letter stating in part:

"You, Mr President, are not declaring a quarantine, but rather are setting forth an ultimatum and threatening that if we do not give in to your demands you will use force. Consider what you are saying! And you want to persuade me to agree to this! What would it mean to agree to these demands? It would mean guiding oneself in one's relations with other countries not by reason, but by submitting to arbitrariness. You are no longer appealing to reason but wish to intimidate us."

October 25

Having knowledge that some missiles in Cuba are operational, the president personally drafts a letter to Premier Khrushchev, again urging him to change the course of events. Meanwhile, Soviet freighters turn and head back to Europe. The Bucharest, carrying only petroleum products, is allowed through the quarantine line. U.N. Secretary-General U Thant calls for a cooling off period, which is rejected by Kennedy because it would leave the missiles in place.

Much public debate between the United States and the Soviet Union takes place in the halls of the United Nations. During the debate in the Security Council, the normally courteous U.S. Ambassador Adlai Stevenson aggressively confronts his Soviet U.N. counterpart Valerian Zorin with photographic evidence of the missiles in Cuba.

October 26

A Soviet-chartered freighter is stopped at the quarantine line and searched for contraband military supplies. None are found; consequently the ship is allowed to proceed to Cuba. Photographic evidence shows accelerated construction of the missile sites and the removal of Soviet IL-28 bombers at Cuban airfields.

In a private letter, Fidel Castro urges Nikita Khrushchev to initiate a nuclear first strike against the United States in the event of an American invasion of Cuba.

Aleksander Fomin of the Soviet embassy staff approaches John Scali, an ABC News reporter, with a proposal for a solution to the crisis.

Later, a long, rambling letter from Khrushchev to Kennedy makes a similar offer: removal of the missiles in exchange for lifting the quarantine and a pledge that the U.S. will not invade Cuba.

October 27

A second letter from Moscow demanding tougher terms, including the removal of Jupiter missiles from Turkey, is received in Washington. In the meantime, over Cuba, an American U-2 plane is shot down by a Soviet-supplied surface-to-air missile. Unfortunately the pilot, Major Rudolph Anderson, is killed. President Kennedy writes a letter to the widow of USAF Major Rudolf Anderson, Jr., offering condolences, and informing her that he will be awarding her husband the Distinguished Service Medal, posthumously.

At a tense meeting of the Executive Committee, President Kennedy resists pressure for immediate military action against the SAM sites. At several points in the discussion, Kennedy insists that removal of the American missiles in Turkey would have to be part of an overall negotiated settlement.

The Committee ultimately decides to ignore the Saturday letter from Moscow and respond favourably to the more conciliatory Friday message. Air Force troop carrier squadrons are ordered to active duty in case an invasion is required.

Later that night, Robert Kennedy meets secretly with Ambassador Anatoly Dobrynin. They reach a basic understanding: the Soviet Union will withdraw the missiles from Cuba under United Nations supervision in exchange for an American pledge not to invade Cuba. In an additional secret understanding, the United States agrees to eventually remove the Jupiter missiles from Turkey.

October 28

The thirteen days marking the most dangerous period of the Cuban missile crisis ends. Radio Moscow announces that the Soviet Union has accepted the proposed solution and releases the text of a Khrushchev letter affirming that the missiles will be removed in exchange for a non-invasion pledge from the United States.

IMMEDIATE RELEASE   October 28, 1962

Office of the White House Press Secretary
- -

THE WHITE HOUSE

STATEMENT BY THE PRESIDENT

I welcome Chairman Khrushchev's statesmanlike decision to stop building
bases in Cuba, dismantling offensive weapons and returning them to the Soviet
Union under United Nations verification. This is an important and construc-
tive contribution to peace.

We shall be in touch with the Secretary General of the United Nations with
respect to reciprocal measures to assure peace in the Caribbean area.

It is my earnest hope that the governments of the world can, with a solution
of the Cuban crisis, turn their urgent attention to the compelling necessity
for ending the arms race and reducing world tensions. This applies to the
military confrontation between the Warsaw Pact and NATO countries as
well as to other situations in other parts of the world where tensions lead
to the wasteful diversion of resources to weapons of war.

# # # # # # # #

While the world almost came to an end the song topping the Billboard charts was
Monster Mash *by Bobby Picket and the Crypt Kickers.*

This was followed by He's a Rebel *by The Crystals*

COSMONAUTS WEAR PRADA

CHAPTER 9

April 12, 1961

While the Americans were still gloating over Ham's successful mission, the Soviets launched the first man into space, Yuri Gagarin. This could be argued as the most significant event in space travel ever.

Yuri Gagarin

Los Angles 1961

The Spanish Bar & Restaurant

'Can you believe these fucking Russians, Bob? I honestly didn't think they were that smart. They've beaten us at every milestone in space and now they've got some fellow orbiting the Earth.'

'Look at the TV, Rick, he's landed back on Earth and he looks fine. The bastard is waving to the fucking world.'

'I feel sick.'

White House Washington

'I don't believe it. We are a bee's dick away from sending our man into space and the Russians pipped us again,' said President Kennedy.

'Don't worry, we'll be first at something significant soon. The important thing is next month we will launch a man into space,' said Vice President Johnson.

'Nothing better go wrong. I couldn't stand it.'

May 5, 1961

US Fighter Pilot Alan Shepard was launched into space aboard Freedom 7. He was the first pilot to land still in his spacecraft.

Alan Shepard

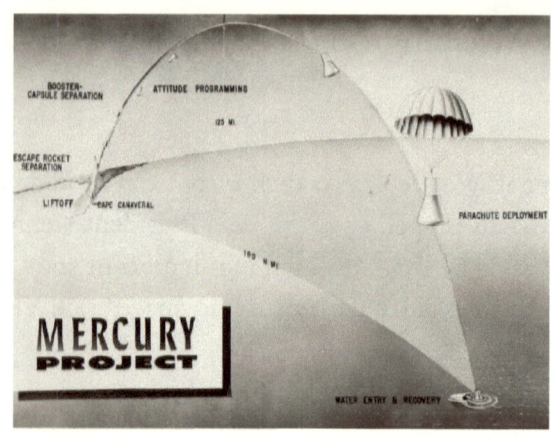

The Trajectory

Los Angles, 1961

The Spanish Bar & Restaurant

'We may not have been first, Rick, but it still feels pretty good.'
'Yeah, I'm with you, Bob.'

White House, Washington

May 1961

'What a magnificent achievement, Mr President. I think all Americans should feel very proud,' said LBJ.

'Yes, Lyndon. I for one am proud to be American. I would like you to arrange for Captain Shepard to meet me here in the Oval Office.'

Fort Bliss Texas

Wernher von Braun, his brother Magnus and the entire Redstone team looked on in awe as their rocket lifted Alan Shepherd into a suborbital flight.

They all cheered and slapped each other on the back. Now they were on their way to discovering space.

'You must be very proud, Wernher,' said Magnus.

'I am, as you should be… in fact everybody in the team.'

'Now we go to the next step and put a man into orbit then, who knows… maybe the moon.'

August 6, 1962

Russian cosmonaut Gherman Titov was launched into space. He orbited the Earth for a full day. The purpose of such a prolonged flight was to study the effects of weightlessness on the human body. He orbited Earth over 17 times; a magnificent achievement compared to Alan Shepherd's suborbital flight the previous year.

1962; The Beatles Were Launched

Love Me Do was released worldwide. Their debut single reached number one in four countries including the United States. Ironically, it only reached number 17 in the UK.

The next ten years of the Beatles was as significant as the Space Race.

The Beatles became the best-selling group in music history, with sales topping 800 million records worldwide. They sold 178 million records in the USA alone. In their native UK they had released more number one albums than any other band, and the same applied to singles.

The Beatles were inducted into the Rock and Roll Hall of Fame in 1988, as were the individual members over the following thirty years.

They received many awards, including an Academy Award and seven Grammy Awards.

Beatles 1962

Beatles 1972

Dec 17, 1960 - First British performance as the Beatles, at the Casbah Coffee Club, Liverpool.

Jan 1, 1962 - They audition for Decca records but are turned down because "groups of guitars are on the way out". Record shop owner Brian Epstein becomes their manager.

June 6, 1962 - First recording session at EMI with George Martin as producer.

Oct. 1962 - *Love Me Do*, their first single as the Beatles, enters the British chart and reaches number 17.

Jan. 1963 - *Please Me* reaches Number One in four of the five British singles charts, beginning a sequence of 12 consecutive number ones.

Feb. 11, 1963 - Recording of their first album, *Please Please Me*, is completed in one day.

Nov. 1963 - *With the Beatles* becomes the first million-selling album in Britain.

Feb. 7-22, 1964 - the Beatles tour the United States for the first time, and they break TV viewing records on the Ed Sullivan Show.

July 6, 1964 - Debut film *A Hard Day's Night* premieres. The soundtrack album of the same name is issued on Aug. 10 and reaches number 1. The album contains 13 new songs, some of which were not included in the film.

Dec. 4, 1964 - The fourth album, *Beatles for Sale*, is released, topping the charts immediately.

June 12, 1965 - Queen Elizabeth awards the four the MBE (Member of the British Empire). John returns his in 1969, partly in protest at British support for United States in the Vietnam War.

July 29, 1965 - The second Beatles film, *Help!* premieres. The album is released on Aug. 6 in Britain.

Dec. 3, 1965 - The Beatles start their final British tour. The last live concert in Britain takes place on May 1, 1966. Final concert of all is in San Francisco on Aug. 29, 1966.

Dec. 3, 1965 - *Rubber Soul* is released and sees the group departing from their rock and roll roots for the first time.

Aug 1966 - The *Revolver* album is released.

June 1, 1967 - *Sgt. Pepper's Lonely Hearts Club Band* is released and is British number one for 27 weeks. It becomes the highest selling British album of all time. It is one of the most innovative albums of its time and sounds like a continuous show.

Aug 27, 1967 - Epstein is found dead.

Nov. 27, 1967 – *Magical Mystery Tour* is released in the U.S. as an album and days later as two Extended Play records in Britain. The television film is first shown on Dec. 26, 1967, and it also stars Scottish actor and poet Ivor Cutler.

Jan. 22, 1968 - Apple Corps, a record company founded by the Beatles, opens offices in London.

Feb. 1968 - The group flies to India to meditate with the Maharishi Mahesh Yogi. As divisions appear, for the first time the group works separately on tracks for *The White Album*.

Oct. 1968 - Premiere of animated film *Yellow Submarine*. The album is released in Jan. 1969.

Jan. 1969 - Documentary *Let it Be* is filmed. Intended as an account of Beatles' "rebirth", it chronicles their demise.

May 26-June 2, 1969 - John Lennon and Yoko Ono hold "bed-in" protest at the Hilton Hotel in Amsterdam and record *Give Peace a Chance*.

July/Aug. 1969 – The *Abbey Road* album is recorded - the first recorded solely in stereo. Traffic outside the studio is stopped for the cover photo of the group on a pedestrian crossing. The final mix on August 20 is the last day all four are together in a recording studio. It is released on Sept. 26.

April 1970 - Final studio session for a Beatles record – but with only Ringo Starr there. No formal announcement is made, but news that the Beatles are no more appears on April 10. The thirteenth and last album *Let it Be* is released on May 8 and the film is premiered in London on May 20.

The Beatles' main rivals were the Rolling Stones, who formed in 1962 and recorded 29 studio albums, 13 live albums and 109 singles. With such significant numbers, it's no surprise they sold more than 240 million albums worldwide.

The Rolling Stones 1963

Rolling Stones Now

THE ASSASSINATION

CHAPTER 10

November 21, 1963

President Kennedy, accompanied by his wife Jackie and Vice President Johnson, undertook a two-day, five-city fundraising trip to Texas.

The presidential entourage was warmly received in the first two stops of San Antonio and Houston. They slept in Fort Worth that night.

President Kennedy made a couple of speeches the following morning and then the party flew to Dallas. After the normal meet and greet at Dallas Airport, they boarded a large convertible, sharing the spacious back seat with John Connally, the Texas Governor, and his wife.

They headed for the Trade Mart where Kennedy was scheduled to make yet another speech. The 10-mile route was lined with admirers' 200,000 in all, waving at President Kennedy and Jackie.

As the motorcade turned into Elm Street and headed into Dealey Plaza on the edge of the CBD, the convertible passed the Texas School Book Depository building.

Texas School Book Depository building.

12.20pm

A loud shot rang out. A bullet pierced the base of the President's neck and exited through his throat, going on to pass through the Governor's shoulder and wrist, ultimately lodging in his thigh.

Another bullet was fired, striking President Kennedy in the back of his head. The convertible raced to Parklands Memorial Hospital, but he was pronounced dead on arrival.

The assailant, Lee Harvey Oswald, was quickly arrested, but he never had his day in court as he was shot by Jack Ruby, a distraught supporter of President Kennedy.

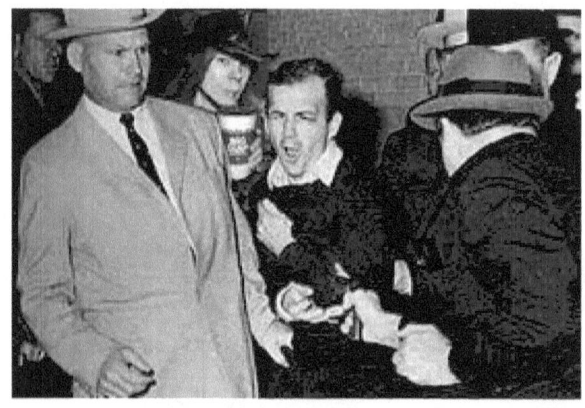

Jack Ruby Shoots Oswald

Jack Ruby

Lyndon Bains Johnson was sworn in as the new president.

LBJ being sworn in. Jackie is wearing the same blood-spattered suit.

Johnson was determined to continue Kennedy's platform of reform.

"The first priority," he said, "is to try to display to the world that we could have continuity and transition, that the program of President Kennedy would be carried on, that there was no need for them to be disturbed and fearful that our constitutional system had been endangered. To demonstrate to the people of this country that although their leader had fallen, and we had a new president, that we must have unity and we must close ranks, and we must work together for the good of all America and the world."

Landing a man on the moon and returning him safely was one of LBJ's high priorities.

June 16, 1963

Valentina Tereshkova became the first woman in space, orbiting the Earth 48 times. The Russian scientists were keen to discover how a woman's body would cope with weightlessness. She passed with flying colours. Her only complaint was that a toothbrush was not included in her kit.

Los Angles, 1963

The Spanish Bar & Restaurant

'For fuck's sake, Bob, we still haven't sent an American into orbit around the Earth. Now, the Russians are sending some dame hurtling around 48 times.'

'Yeah, I know. It's embarrassing.'

Over the next few years, the Soviets continued to prove their superiority. They were clearly winning the space race.

October 12, 1964

The Russians sent three men into orbit; the first time a multi-person crew had been launched into space. Originally only two cosmonauts were allocated a spot, but a medical doctor with strong political connections hitched a ride. The capsule was designed for two, and therefore, something had to be left behind—their space suits.

Cosmonauts Return to Earth in Stylish Outfits

March 18, 1965

Alexey Leonov conducted the first spacewalk, another Russian major achievement.

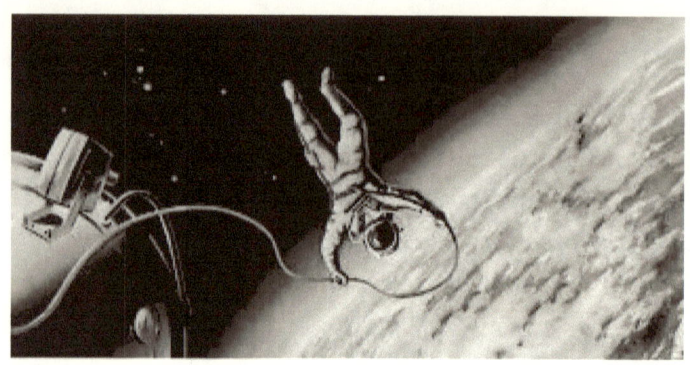

June 3, 1965

The United States launched two astronauts, Ed White and James McDivitt, on a four-day mission. Ed White conducted a twenty-minute spacewalk.

Although seen as a major U.S. accomplishment the Russians had beaten them yet again.

The United States prioritised space exploration. Their objective was not only the moon; they wanted to discover the planets in our solar system.

July 14, 1965

The Mariner satellite passed Mars at the closest point ever. The photos it took and transmitted back to Earth dismissed the possibility of life on the planet.

The Surface of Mars

White House, Washington

'Well, Mars isn't what I thought. The whole planet is a desert,' said President Johnson.

'I agree. I expected to see some camels.'

'Don't be ridiculous, Hubert.'

'What's our next mission?'

'Two astronauts are going up for eight days, which will give us the record.'

'Excellent. It's about time we got one up on the Russians.'

The huge Gemini rocket designed and built by von Braun and his team lifted off on August 29, 1965.

Two crewmen were aboard, Gordon Cooper and Pete Conrad, and they orbited the Earth 120 times.

Tragedy

The Apollo program changed forever on Jan. 27, 1967, when a flash fire swept through the Apollo 1 command module during a launch rehearsal test. The three men inside perished despite the best efforts of the ground crew. It would take more than 18 months, and extensive redesigns, before NASA sent more men into space.

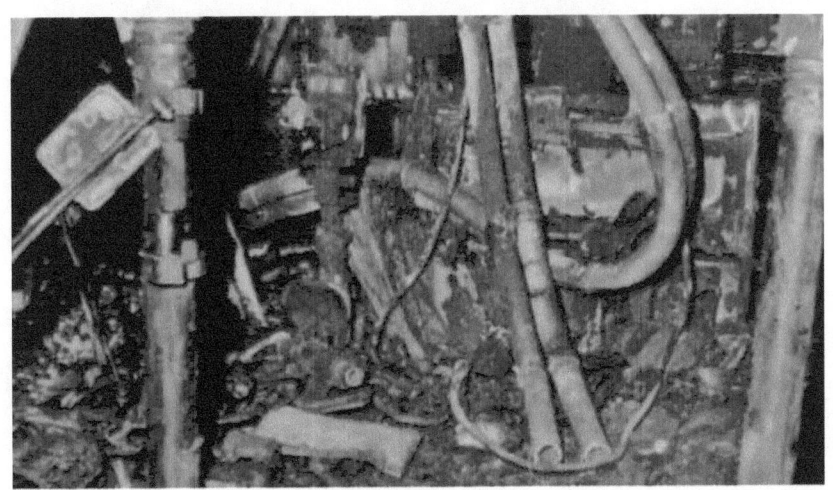

Burnt out capsule

Gus Grissom, Ed White, Roger B. Chaffee

The Arizona Daily Star

Apollo Training Craft Explodes

ASTRONAUTS DIE IN FIERY CAPSULE

Three-Man Crew Killed Instantly

President Johnson did not try to interfere with the investigation. It was NASA's responsibility to determine the cause of the fire.

The most critical finding was the danger of using pure oxygen in the capsule. It was a disaster waiting to happen. It made the capsule lighter, but much more volatile.

The next eighteen months were spent redesigning and constructing the new capsule. Only 34% oxygen was used. This required a much thicker capsule wall to handle the pressure. The new design became the standard for all future manned space flights.

At last, the Apollo moon project got underway again with Apollo 7.

Apollo 7 Landed Safely

BRILLIANCE IS NOT A COLOUR

CHAPTER 11

Katherine Johnson nee Coleman was enjoying the celebration of her niece's birthday in Hampton Virginia. Her siblings were all present, as were her mother and father. Several friends and relatives had also been invited to the party including Nancy, Katherine's cousin.

'How are you enjoying teaching, Katherine?' asked Nancy.

'I'm enjoying it. The kids are great, but I don't feel I'm using my qualifications to full advantage.'

'Have you thought of changing careers?'

'Nancy, we both know how difficult it is for a black woman in the workforce. The opportunities are very limited.'

'I heard the National Advisory Committee for Aeronautics (NACA) are looking to recruit black mathematicians.'

'You mean only black women are being hired?'

'No, white as well. My point is they are not excluding us.'

'Do you know if they're still hiring?'

'I don't know. Why don't you contact them?'

Katherine applied and was granted an interview. She was offered a position as a mathematician, and she began working at NACA in 1952. She was assigned a role in the Guidance and Navigation Department in 1953.

Initially, Katherine performed complex maths together with a group of female mathematicians. They were known as "virtual computers who wore skirts." The male engineers considered the woman below them. They ate their meals at separate tables.

Their role was to decipher data from black boxes carried on planes, but they also performed other complex mathematical tasks.

Katherine and a fellow worker were approached to join the all-male flight research team, a very elite group. Although it was a temporary assignment it was regarded as a great honour. The two women were masters of analytic geometry; a skill that was required in the department. Katherine and Betty became indispensable and never returned to the women's pool.

They had to contend with both gender and racial barriers but the women just ignored them and got on with their work.

Editorial meetings were strictly the domain of the men. Katherine insisted on attending on the premise that she had done the work and therefore should be part of the group. She got her way, which continued throughout her career.

Johnson worked as a "computer" from 1953 to 1958, analysing gust alleviation and other complex topics. Her supervisor was Dorothy Vaughn, renowned as a brilliant mathematician. Katherine was eventually assigned to the Guidance and Control Division located at Langley. Here she had to contend with not only being the only woman but also the only black person.

When NACA was disbanded a new organisation was created. Named NASA, it adopted digital computers, which replaced much of the mathematical work Katherine and her colleagues had completed. The other major change was desegregating the workforce.

'We needed to be assertive as women in those days – assertive and aggressive – and the degree to which we had to be that way depended on where you were. I had to be. In the early days of NASA, women were not allowed to put their names on the reports – no woman in my division had had her name on a report. I was working with Ted Skopinski and he wanted to leave and go to Houston... but Henry Pearson, our supervisor – he was not a fan of women – kept pushing him to finish the report we were working on. Finally, Ted told him, "Katherine should finish the report. She's done most of the work anyway." So Ted left Pearson with no choice; I finished the report, and my name went on it, and that was the first time a woman in our division had her name on something.'

Katherine Johnson's House

Johnson's career continued to develop. As an aerospace technologist she calculated the trajectory for Alan Shepard's space flight. He was the first American in space.

Her most critical task was plotting the backup navigation charts for astronauts in case of electronic failures.

NASA began to depend on digital computers to calculate the orbit around the Earth, but they were used only when Johnson verified the calculations. John Glenn refused to fly without Johnson's verifications, which included gravitational pulls of celestial bodies— very complex calculations.

John Glenn became a household name and the black woman who was instrumental in achieving his orbit remained anonymous.

$$\text{Out[70]=} \left(-2c^4y^2 - 2a^4z^2 - 2c^2\left(\text{ArcSin}\left[\frac{\sqrt{a^2-c^2}}{\sqrt{\kappa+a^2}}\right]\sqrt{\kappa+a^2}\sqrt{\frac{a^2-c^2}{\kappa+a^2}}\sqrt{(\kappa+a^2)^2(\kappa+c^2)}+\kappa y^2-\kappa z^2\right)+\right.$$

$$\sqrt{(\kappa+a^2)^2(\kappa+c^2)}\left(\left(-\text{ArcSin}\left[\frac{\sqrt{a^2-c^2}}{\sqrt{\kappa+a^2}}\right]\sqrt{\kappa+a^2}\sqrt{\frac{a^2-c^2}{\kappa+a^2}}+\sqrt{a^2-c^2}\sqrt{\frac{(a^2-c^2)(\kappa+c^2)}{(\kappa+a^2)^2}}\right)x^2-\right.$$

$$\left(\text{ArcSin}\left[\frac{\sqrt{a^2-c^2}}{\sqrt{\kappa+a^2}}\right]\sqrt{\kappa+a^2}\sqrt{\frac{a^2-c^2}{\kappa+a^2}}+\sqrt{a^2-c^2}\sqrt{\frac{(a^2-c^2)(\kappa+c^2)}{(\kappa+a^2)^2}}\right)y^2+$$

$$2\,\text{ArcSin}\left[\frac{\sqrt{a^2-c^2}}{\sqrt{\kappa+a^2}}\right]\sqrt{\kappa+a^2}\sqrt{\frac{a^2-c^2}{\kappa+a^2}}\,z^2\right)+$$

$$\left.2a^2\left(\text{ArcSin}\left[\frac{\sqrt{a^2-c^2}}{\sqrt{\kappa+a^2}}\right]\sqrt{\kappa+a^2}\sqrt{\frac{a^2-c^2}{\kappa+a^2}}\sqrt{(\kappa+a^2)^2(\kappa+c^2)}+(\kappa+c^2)y^2+(-\kappa+c^2)z^2\right)\right)\Big/$$

$$\left(2(a^2-c^2)^2\sqrt{(\kappa+a^2)^2(\kappa+c^2)}\right)$$

A Johnson Formula

Katherine adopted the digital computer, becoming proficient in programming these machines. It was she who helped locate Alan Shepard's capsule after his historic flight, using the trajectory she calculated.

Alan Shepard's Space Capsule being recovered

Johnson's most important work was in relation to the Apollo 11 moonwalk.

It was Katherine's calculations that were instrumental in determining the trajectory for Apollo 11.

Her most famous work related to Apollo 13. When the moon landing was aborted, she developed the backup procedures and charts that helped set a safe path for the three-man crew to return to Earth safely.

Johnson regarded this as her most important work, not Apollo 11.

Katherine worked on the Space Shuttle program and various unmanned missions to Mars.

How did Katherine Johnson a black woman growing up in a segregated America, achieve such amazing things?

Katherine Johnson

MATHS IS FUN

CHAPTER 12

The young Afro American girl was waiting for the bus to take her to school. There were several other black kids waiting in the bus shelter. Katherine saw the yellow bus first and got up quickly, hoping to get the front seat. She was disappointed to discover it was a white only bus. She and the other kids would have to wait.

Black Only Bus

Ten minutes later the black and coloured bus arrived.

Segregation didn't worry Katherine; her only concern was attending school and learning as much as she could as quickly as she could. Her main love was mathematics. She would count things before she could walk.

Segregated Schoolroom

Katherine excelled at school and by the time she turned 10 she was ready to begin her secondary education. Unfortunately, there were no schools in White Sulphur Springs willing to take a black student so her only option was to move. The family made a tough decision. Joshua would stay and work in the timber industry in White Sulphur Springs while Joylette would take Katherine and her siblings to Institute where they could attend secondary school. The family would join Joshua when the school year ended.

Katherine graduated from high school at the age of 14 and then attended college; West Virginia State. She was a dedicated student, taking every maths course available to her. Tutors such as Angie Turner King and W. W. Schieffelin mentored her. Johnson graduated summa cum laude (with the highest distinction) with degrees in mathematics and French at the age of 18.

Her first job was teaching.

Her career in aeronautics began soon after.

I AIN'T GOING TO SPEND MY LIFE BEING A COLOUR

MICHAEL JACKSON

February 4, 1913

John A. Andrew Memorial Hospital
Tuskegee Alabama

Rosa Parks was born to James and Leona McCauley in John A. Andrew Memorial Hospital, a designated black hospital in the segregated South. The marriage was a troubled one and when Rosa was two years old her parents separated. Leona moved the family to Pine Level, Alabama, to live with her parents.

Rosa's grandparents had been slaves and it was their influence that taught the young Rosa the need for racial equality. The family home was situated on a farm where crops were grown and sold at the markets.

Rosa never forgot seeing the Ku Klux Klan march past their house en route to a rally. Her grandfather stood on the front lawn with a loaded shotgun, staring down the hooded thugs.

Rosa completed high school where she was regarded as an A grade student, but with the family's limited finances she was unable to attend a black college to further her studies. She secured a job at the Montgomery Department Store as a seamstress.

December 1, 1955

After a particularly long day, Rosa boarded the Cleveland Avenue bus, looking forward to going home.

The bus was segregated just like all the buses in Montgomery. A sign was placed designating white from black. Rosa took her place in the first row of the coloured seats.

Montgomery bus drivers had police powers while in charge of a bus. When a black passenger boarded the bus it would be via the front door, but they were required to exit via the back door. If they disobeyed this rule they could be arrested.

The bus continued on its route. Some passengers got off while more got on and eventually the driver realised there were several white passengers standing in the aisle. He stopped the bus, moved the sign separating the black and white sections and instructed four black passengers to vacate their seats so that the white passengers could sit down. Three obeyed without complaint but Rosa refused to give up her seat. Under Montgomery law, if a black person refused to give up their seat for a white person the driver could call the police and have them removed or worse still arrest them.

'I asked you to move, lady. Why won't you do as I say?'
'I don't think I should have to stand up.'
'I'm going to call the police. They'll make you stand up.'
The driver called the police and they arrested Rosa. Later Rosa recalled that she was tired of giving in.

She was charged with a violation of Chapter 6, Section 11 of the Montgomery City Code. The police took Rosa to police headquarters and placed her in a cell. She was released on bail later that night.

Rosa's Mug Shot

Word of Rosa's arrest spread among the black community. Mr E D Nixon, head of the local chapter of the **National Association for the Advancement of Coloured People, NAACP**, decided enough was enough and began to organise a boycott of the Montgomery City buses.

The campaign began, ads were placed in all the local papers and distributed throughout the black neighbourhoods.

A call to action was made to boycott the buses on Monday December 5, 1955, the day of Rosa's trial. The black community were encouraged to avoid going to work and the children were kept home from school.

On the morning of December 5, a group of leaders from NAACP got together to map out their strategy on how best to exploit the opportunity. They decided a new organisation was required with powerful leadership.

The new group would be called the Montgomery Improvement Association. The members voted for a new community member, Martin Luther King, the minister of the Dexter Avenue Baptist Church, to be their leader. They intended to use the Rosa Parks case to create real change in race relations.

Martin Luther King

Rosa arrived at the Montgomery County Courthouse with her lawyer, Fred Gray. She looked up at the magnificent yet imposing building which she had passed many times but which she had never entered.

A crowd of over 500 was outside, waiting to support her.

She climbed the steps quickly, a look of determination on her face. She was not intimidated by the occasion.

Her lawyer guided her to the seat she was required to occupy. The judge entered, the court all stood, and the trial got underway. It lasted 30 minutes.

Rosa was found guilty and fined $10 plus a $4 court fee. The guilty verdict infuriated the black community and, consequently, the boycott continued.

After 381 days it came to a halt. By then. the Montgomery Bus Boycott was entrenched into the civil rights history books. Rosa Parks became a household name not just in America but also around the world.

Rosa Parks

I Have a Dream

Chapter 13

Martin Luther King Jr. was born on January 15, 1929, in Atlanta Georgia, as the middle child of Michael King Sr. and Alberta King. Both Michael's and Alberta's families were well established in Georgia.

King's birth name was Michael King; the same name as his father's, but Michael Senior changed his and young Michael's names to Martin Luther after attending the Baptist World Alliance in Germany in 1934. Martin Luther became Michael Senior's inspiration.

Martin Luther – 1483-1546

King's father persuaded the birth registrar that the name on his son's birth certificate was a mistake and it was changed to Martin Luther King Jr. in 1957.

Atlanta, 1934

Young Michael King was throwing his brand-new baseball against a brick wall near his house. He would throw it and try to catch it his efforts weren't always successful.

A white boy named John approached him.

'If you keep throwing that ball against the wall you'll ruin it.'
'I know, but I've got no one to play ball with.'
'I'll play with you if you like.'
'That would be great. What's your name?'
'John. What's yours?'
'Michael, I live just down the road from you.'
'Yeah, I know. I've seen you before.'
The two five-year-olds became great friends, playing ball in the summer and football in the fall.

When Michael and John turned six they were required to start school. Unfortunately, Michael had to attend a school for African Americans while John attended a public white school.

John came home from school one day and was surprised to find his father waiting for him.

'John, I don't want you playing with that black kid today, in fact, I don't want you playing with him again.'
'Why Dad? He's my best friend.'
'Not any more he's not. He's different. In case you haven't noticed he's black and you're white.'
That was the end of a beautiful friendship and the beginning of Martin Luther Jr.'s depression.

King suffered depression throughout his life. It was caused by several factors, including racial segregation. At the age of 12 he tried to commit suicide by jumping out of a second storey window, but fortunately he survived.

King attended the Booker T Washington High School where he established a reputation for his public speaking ability and became a key member of the debating team.

Booker T Washington High School

During his junior year, he won first prize in an oratorical contest sponsored by the Negro Elks Club in Dublin Georgia.

The accomplishment was soured while] returning to Atlanta by bus.

The bus driver approached King and his teacher where they were sitting midway down the bus.

'You two get up and let these white folks sit down.'
'We were here first, so why should we stand?' protested King.
'Because they're white and you're black, boy.'
'That's not fair. I'm not moving.'
'I think we better do as he says, Martin, or they could have us arrested,' said Mr Armstrong, Martin's teacher.
Reluctantly, Martin and Armstrong gave their seats up for the white passengers.

King was furious and never forgot the incident. He went on to be an outstanding student, skipping both the 9th and 12th grades.

King was accepted as an undergraduate at Morehouse College, a respected black university, when he was only fifteen. He graduated at the young age of nineteen with a BA in sociology and made the critical decision to enter the ministry where he felt he could serve humanity.

King enrolled to study for a BA in divinity at Crozer Theological Seminary in Pennsylvania he graduated at the age of twenty-two in 1951.

King commenced his doctorate studies in systematic theology at Boston University, where he received his PhD on June 5th, 1955.

This was the same year as the Montgomery Bus Boycott and established Martin Luther King as a national spokesman for the civil rights movement.

Time Line of Martin Luther King's life as an activist.

1955

The 26-year-old King leads boycott of segregated Montgomery buses, gains national reputation.

1956

King's house is bombed

U.S. Supreme Court ruling prompts Montgomery to desegregate buses.

1957

King helps found the Southern Christian Leadership Conference (SCLC).

1958

Writes *Stride Towards Freedom*, about the bus boycott.

1959

Visits India to study nonviolence and **civil disobedience.**

1960

Joins his father as co-pastor of Ebenezer Baptist Church in Atlanta.

1963

King is arrested and jailed during anti-segregation protests in Birmingham; writes *Letter From Birmingham City Jail*, arguing that individuals have the moral duty to disobey unjust laws

Delivers "I Have a Dream" speech during the March on Washington attended by 200,000 protesters, creates a powerful image, builds momentum for civil rights legislation.

1964

Publishes *Why We Can't Wait*

Congress passes the Civil Rights Act of 1964, outlawing segregation in public accommodations and discrimination in education and employment.

King receives the **Nobel Peace Prize.**

1965

King and SCLC join the voting-rights march from **Selma** to Montgomery; police beat and tear gas marchers; King addresses rally before state capitol, builds support for voting rights.

Congress passes the Voting Rights Act of 1965, which suspends (later bans) literacy tests and other restrictions to prevent blacks from voting.

Mid-1960s

King's growing opposition to the Vietnam War angers President Johnson, and prompts many white activists to switch to anti-war activities.

1966

Growing popularity of the black power movement, with blacks stressing self-reliance and self-defence, indicates King's influence was declining, especially among young blacks.

King turns towards economic issues; SCLC moves civil rights struggle to the North; opens Chicago office to organize protests against housing and employment discrimination.

1967

King plans Poor People's Campaign; advocates redistribution of wealth to eradicate black poverty.

Publishes *Where Do We Go from Here: Chaos or Community?*

1968

King is assassinated in Memphis, during a visit to support striking black garbage collectors; violent riots erupt in more than 100 U.S. cities.

by David Johnson

WEAR A FLOWER IN YOUR HAIR

CHAPTER 14

January 12, 1966

David Porter and Melanie Andres had been an item for the past year. Both were students at Ohio State University. David was studying Business while Melanie was studying Sociology. They met at the university's library and had been inseparable since.

'Why don't we go and see a movie tonight Dave,' said Melanie.

'Sure, why not, what movie did you have in mind?'
'*A Man for all Seasons*. I read the play in High School.'
'I was rather hoping you would say *Alfie*. I've heard it's really good.'
They compromised and chose *Who's Afraid of Virginia Wolf.*

Life on the campus was pretty good for Dave and Melanie and both were excellent students. They mixed in an interesting, albeit eclectic, circle of friends.

One of their friends was Jimmie White, who came from a very wealthy farming family. He drove a Corvette and always dressed in designer clothes. Jimmie was studying Agricultural Science on the basis that he would one day take over the farm. His nickname was the Gentleman Farmer.

At the end of the final semester, Jimmie drove to California to discover the Golden State. He drove the full length of the state, finishing in San Francisco. He was keen to see a few of the hippy freaks he had read about.

He returned to Ohio three weeks later a changed man. He sold the Corvette and purchased a VW Kombi Van. He paid the local panel works shop to paint the entire van with a psychedelic design.

Jimmie's Corvette

Jimmie's VW Kombi Van

'What's going on with you, Jimmie?' asked David.

'Man, I have discovered the real me. I've been living a materialistic life, not really caring about other people or the environment we live in. I'm moving to San Francisco to become a flower child, a hippy.'

'Fuck, man, that's a big move. What about your studies?'

'I'm dropping out.'

'Have you told your parents?'

'Yep, they'll get over it. My younger brother can take over the ranch.'

'You're giving up a lot, Jimmie. Are you sure you know what you're doing?'

'Dave, I'm giving up a whole lot of materialistic bullshit. It no longer means anything to me. You and Melanie should come over for a visit once I'm settled.

'Okay, you take care, friend.'

'I will.'

Jimmie took off on his long trip the next day. His intention was to drive eight hours a day with rest stops every two hours. He estimated the journey would take him eight days. He estimated correctly, and he drove through Golden Gate Park at the end of the eighth day. His destination was Scott Street in the Haight Ashbury area. The Kaliflower Commune was located there. Jimmie had met several commune members on his previous trip to San Francisco. He checked out of his hotel and stayed in the commune for five days. It was this experience that convinced him to join the commune.

Scott Street Commune House

Jimmie walked in the front door and was greeted by several of the hippies.

'Hey man, you made it— you came back,' said Cosmic Tim.

'Yeah, I said I'd be back.'

'You can join our marriage group if you like, Jimmie. There's ten in the group and we all share our love,' said Wendy.

'I'd love to.'

Members of the Kaliflower Commune

The Kaliflower Commune centred around cooperation among its members. It was like one big happy family. The commune members rarely mixed with non-commune people.

Any savings a member had acquired were given to the commune. They were also encouraged to quit their jobs and work inside the community. The tasks included gardening, cleaning, cooking and working in the free print shop.

Jimmie had dropped out, so he was free to work with the other commune members.

Major decisions were made by consensus within the daily meeting of community members. The commune also held voluntary criticism sessions to vent concerns with other commune members. During such a session, the member who asked for criticism would invite other members to participate, and then listen in silence while concerns and criticisms were aired. Usually the member did not respond for three days. This system of self-governance was borrowed from the 19th-century American Utopian community at Oneida, NY.

'Hey, Jimmie, are you going to the *Human Be–In* at Golden Gate Park on January 14?' asked Wendy.

'I'm not sure.'

'You can't miss out on the greatest event of the century.

Anybody who's anybody will be playing, including The Mamas & the Papas, The Grateful Dead, Jefferson Airplane— everybody.'

'Will everybody from the commune be going?'

'You bet.'

'Okay, you've talked me into it although the idea of 30,000 people in a park doesn't turn me on.'

Turn On, Tune In, Drop Out

TIMOTHY LEARY

The day was perfect; blue sky with a gentle breeze coming from the bay. People were filling the vast grass area of the polo ground and it appeared the forecasted numbers would be accurate.

The first act to blow everybody away was The Grateful Dead, followed by Quicksilver Messenger, Jefferson Airplane, Big Brother and the Holding Company and many more bands.

Grateful Dead

Jefferson Airplane

Janis Joplin & Big Brother and the Holding Company

The organisers promised one million LSD tabs would be given away. Judging by the behaviour of a large section of the crowd, many took advantage, including the Kaliflower members. The sound of the bands permeated to the very edge of the field, hippies were dancing slowly, and the smell of marijuana wafted over the crowd. It was a very primeval scene.

'How good was Janis! That girl's got a voice,' said Wendy.

'Yeah, she can certainly belt it out,' said Jimmie.

The members returned to the commune and continued to smoke dope. Many couples disappeared to make love. It was a great day.

Janis Joplin

MONTEREY

CALIFORNIA DREAMING

CHAPTER 15

1967

A decade into the space race, Russia achieved another first; two Soviet spacecraft made the first fully automated space docking in the history of space exploration on October 30, 1967. Mutual search, approach, mooring, and docking was automatically performed by the IGLA-system on board Kosmos 186. After 3.5 hours of joint flight, the satellites parted on a command sent from the Earth and continued to orbit separately. Officially, both made a soft landing in a predetermined region of the Soviet Union - Kosmos 186 on October 31, 1967, and Kosmos 188 on November 2, 1967.

Ten years earlier, Sputnik was launched... a satellite the size of a beach ball. The Russian space program had come a long way.

Kosmos 186 and 188 about to dock

In the same year the Russian satellite docking took place the Monterey Pop Festival was held in California. It was a first for the USA.

Sarah Henderson worked for NASA as an IT Specialist. Her boyfriend Mike Baker was an Aerospace Engineer. Sarah was twenty-four and Mike was twenty-six. They had been going out for the past two years.

They were both located at NASA's Ames Research Centre in Mountain View California.

Ames Research Centre

'Hey, Sarah, do you want to go to the Monterey Pop Festival? It should be fantastic based on the acts they've got playing.'

'Sounds like fun. Let's do it.'

'Great, it starts on June 16 and ends on the 18th.'

'So, who's playing?'

'Yes, they are.'

Beg your pardon.'

'Sorry, just kidding. The Who is one of the bands playing.'

'Come on, which bands are playing?'

'I've got the playlist here. Take a look.'

Friday, June 16, 1967

Beverley Martyn

Eric Burdon & the Animals

Johnny Rivers

Lou Rawls

Simon & Garfunkel

The Association

The Paupers

Saturday, June 17, 1967

Al Kooper

Big Brother and The Holding Company

Booker T. & The M.G.'s

Canned Heat

Country Joe and the Fish

Hugh Masekela

Jefferson Airplane

Laura Nyro

Moby Grape

Otis Redding

Quicksilver Messenger Service

Steve Miller Band

The Byrds

The Electric Flag

The Paul Butterfield Blues Band

Sunday, June 18, 1967

Big Brother and The Holding Company

Buffalo Springfield

Cyrus Faryar

Grateful Dead

Ravi Shankar

The Blues Project

The Jimi Hendrix Experience

The Mamas & the Papas

The Who

'Unbelievable! What a line-up! Pity the Beatles aren't playing.'
'Apparently, Paul McCartney was at Mama Cass's house with John and
Michelle Phillips when they all came up with the idea for the festival.'

'Really? So why aren't the Beatles headlining?'

'Their music has become too complex to play live is supposed to be the reason.'

'And what about the Rolling Stones?'

'I don't know why they're not playing although I heard Brian Jones will be there.'

'Well, it's a huge line-up so it'll be fun.'

PEACE & LOVE

AND

PLENTY OF DRUGS

CHAPTER 16

Friday 16 June 1967

Sarah and Mike commenced their road trip to Monterey at 8am, trying to beat the traffic. Unfortunately, there were many others who had the same thought. Instead of taking two hours it ended up a four-hour journey from San Francisco. Mike knew the road well, for he had driven it many times. Once they reached the fairgrounds, they used the pre-paid pass to park the Kombi in the car park.

Mike found a suitable parking spot not too far from the amenities, and once set up, they decided to take a walk and check out the stage and the venue itself.

As they strolled through the grounds they bumped into Anne Benson, Sarah's next-door neighbour.

'Hi, you guys, is this going to be unbelievable or what?'

'With the bands playing how could it not be?' said Sarah.

The couple said goodbye and continued their walk of discovery. They wandered through the stalls selling everything from mystical books, flowers, music and other things… not all of them legal. Sarah decided to get a flower painted in bright colours on each cheek to get into the mood of the festival.

The food stalls were the next port of call. Mike knew they would have no chance of getting something to eat once the concert began. Two pastrami rolls and two Cokes would satisfy their appetites.

The first act, The Association, was due to step on stage at 7 pm so they returned to the Kombi to retrieve some things including a few joints, and then they headed for their seats in front of the stage.

John Phillips from The Mamas & the Papas walked on stage at 7.05. He was one of the people who conceived the idea to hold the festival. Papa John welcomed the huge crowd and then introduced The Association.

All six members were dressed in suits and ties; this was not the standard dress during the remainder of the festival. They started their gig with, *Enter the Young*, followed by *Along Comes Mary*, and finished with their hit single *Windy*.

The Association

The crowd was warming up. It was going to be a long night full of music, dancing, and weed.

Monterey Crowd

By the time Eric Burdon and the Animals walked on stage at 9 pm, Sarah and Mike had smoked two joints and consumed their pastrami roles. They were mellow.

Eric Burdon - San Franciscan Nights

Chet Helms, Big Brother and the Holding Company's manager and the promoter who infused Janis Joplin into the band introduced Eric Burdon and the Animals, the only British band to play on Friday night.

Chet Helms Introducing Eric Burdon

Eric Burdon began:

This following program is dedicated to the city and people of San Francisco.
Who may not know it but they are beautiful

And so is their city. This is a very personal song
So if the viewer cannot understand it

Particularly those of you who are European residents
Save up all your bread and fly Trans Love Airways to San Francisco U.S.A.
Then maybe you'll understand the song, it will be worth it
If not for the sake of this song but for the sake of your own peace of mind.

The song *Warm San Franciscan Night* began.

This was the first time Eric Burden and The Animals performed the song in public, having written it in San Francisco only a few days before.

Following Monterey, it went to number one in Canada and reached number nine in the USA. It also reached number seven in the UK.

The huge crowd loved it as did the other band members standing in the wings, including Paul Simon and Art Garfunkel, who were the last act to perform for the night.

It was now time for Simon & Garfunkel; John Phillips introduced them as one of the greatest duos of all time.

The music began. The crowd knew it was *Homeward Bound,* and many stood and danced to the familiar sound.

The Sounds of Silence and *The 59ᵗʰ Street Bridge Song* (Feelin' Groovy) were the favourites.

The last song for the day was *Punky's Dilemma*, and then the throng gradually vacated the arena and grandstands, either heading home or to the camping area. Saturday was going to be a huge day.

Saturday, June 17, 1967

Canned Heat

Big Brother and The Holding Company

Al Kooper

Booker T. & The M.G.'s

Country Joe and the Fish

Hugh Masekela

Jefferson Airplane

Laura Nyro

Moby Grape

Otis Redding

Quicksilver Messenger Service

Steve Miller Band

The Byrds

The Electric Flag

The Paul Butterfield Blues Band

Janis Joplin with Big Brother and the Holding Company

The next group on stage was Big Brother and the Holding Company featuring Janis Joplin.

The band started their gig with *Down on Me*, and that got the crowd's attention. The finale was *Ball and Chain*. It brought the house down, launching Janis Joplin into super-stardom.

Saturday night gave Grace Slick and Jefferson Airplane their opportunity to impress the crowd. Jerry Garcia from the Grateful Dead introduced the group.

They began their eight-song gig with *Somebody to Love* and finished with *The Ballad of You and Me* and *Pooneil*.

Jefferson Airplane was one of the groups with which the huge audience was very familiar; they were regarded as the pioneers of the San Francisco Sound.

A little-known singer called Otis Redding performed the last act for the evening.

If Janis was nervous, Otis was petrified. He was used to performing in front of black audiences in the USA and club audiences in Europe, not 50,000 predominately white hippies from California.

The fact that it was 1am and drizzling rain didn't help Otis's confidence.

His nerves disappeared when he walked out onto the stage, having been introduced by Tommy Smothers; one half of the Smothers Brothers comedy duo.

Otis's backing band Booker T. & the M.G.s started up with *Shake* and Otis's performance won the audience over instantly. He then introduced his next song as the one he gave away to some woman. He then sang *Respect*, which he had penned two years before. Aretha Franklin recorded it only a month before Monterey.

If the crowd weren't enraptured with Otis by then they certainly were after he sang the love ballad *I've Been Loving You Too Long*.

Otis had the audience eating out of his hand and he interacted with the 50,000 as though they were in a small nightclub in Paris.

He got them moving again with a cover of *Satisfaction* and then sent them home to bed with *Try a Little Tenderness*.

Otis Redding had been well and truly discovered by mainstream America.

Otis Redding

Sunday, June 18

When Sarah woke at 9am, Mike was still sound asleep. She wasn't surprised, for they had partied on until 3am.

She opened the Kombi's door, hoping to discover a beautiful morning with bright sunshine. She wasn't disappointed.

Mike stumbled out of the Kombi, looking for a strong coffee.

'Mike, have you heard of that Indian guy? I can't remember his name…'

'You mean Ravi Shankar. Yeah I've heard of him. I believe he's influenced the Beatles quite a bit, and having listened to Sergeant Pepper, I see what they mean,' said Mike.

At 1pm, Ravi Shankar and his Indian musicians assembled on stage. The sound of the sitar began to permeate through the concert arena and, for the next four hours, Ravi Shankar and his accompanying musicians played virtually non-stop.

Some were mesmerised by the Indian music while others had enough after an hour or so and wandered off to partake in other things.

When Ravi Shankar finally concluded his concert, the crowd gave him a standing ovation. Ravi was amazed at the audience reaction. He had never been to a rock festival before and was sceptical that his music would be appreciated at such an event despite getting assurance from George Harrison and the other Beatles.

18 June Sunday Evening

This was to be the final set, a finale to a magnificent festival of music, love and excellent drugs.

Paul Simon walked onto the stage at 7pm to introduce Blues Project.

Their set was short, just two songs; *Flute Thing* and *Wake Me, Shake Me*.

Tommy Smothers walked out to introduce Big Brother and the Holding Company for their second performance.

Janis was not so nervous this time. She knew what to expect… or she thought she did. She decided to wear a *Colin Rose of San Francisco* gold outfit and she certainly stood out from any other female artists performing that night.

By the time Janis and the band had completed *Ball and Chain* to finish their six-song set, the crowd was on their feet shouting for more. Big Brother and the Holding Company had been elevated to the status of a super act.

Jimmie Hendrix was waiting in the Green Room below stage as were the members of The Who and The Mamas & the Papas. An argument broke out between Jimmie, and Pete Townsend from the Who about who would play first; neither wanted to follow the other. It became quite heated until John Phillips intervened, suggesting he tossed a coin. The coin was tossed, Pete called heads and won, so the Who were the next act to go on stage.

Buffalo Springfield finished their six-song set with *Pretty Girl Why*, and Eric Burden walked onto the stage to introduce his fellow Englishmen.

'I would like to introduce you to the Who, a group that will destroy you completely in more ways than one.'

The band exploded into *Substitute*, followed by *Summertime Blues*.

The British group ripped through *Pictures of Lily, A Quick One, While He's Away, Happy Jack,* and *My Generation*. Instead of peace, love and flowers, the Who delivered explosive energetic rock capped off with Townsend using his electric guitar as a massive axe, not only destroying the instrument but some of the other equipment on stage. Keith Moon kicked his drums over and walked off stage. All in all, it was a great day for the music shops.

Who's Destructive?

Only one band could possibly follow such a performance—The Grateful Dead. Jerry Garcia and the boys simply walked on stage and immediately started up with *Viola Lee Blues*, followed by *Cold Rain and Snow*. The final number was *Alligator Caution*. Many commented that it was the purest and best music of the festival, and they were the only act that motivated the crowd to get to their feet and dance.

Brian Jones, founder of the Rolling Stones, walked with Jimmie Hendrix up to the stage where Brian introduced the relatively unknown artist.

'I'd like to introduce a very good friend of mine and the best guitarist I've ever heard—Jimmie Hendrix.'

The first howling sounds of Jimmie's Fender Stratocaster were heard throughout the fairground and beyond where thousands were outside the venue listening to the free concert. The 90,000 inside were in awe as Hendrix launched into *Foxy Lady*, followed by *Like a Rolling Stone, Rock Me Baby, Hey Joe* and *The Wind Cries Mary*. Jimmie had the crowd dumbstruck. They had never heard music like it and when he finished the penultimate song, *Purple Haze*, they were exhausted. They needed all their energy for the final number, *Wild Thing*. It went for nearly eight minutes, and Jimmie demonstrated all his incredible guitar skills before he sacrificed his Stratocaster by setting it alight and then smashing it onstage.

The crowd went berserk, as did his fellow artists watching in the wings…
including the members of the Who.

The only one who showed any disgust was Ravi Shankar.

The final act for the festival was The Mamas & the Papas.

What a contrast! Jimmie Hendrix's burnt-out Stratocaster had been removed
from the stage when Paul Simon introduced the group.

They began their set with *Straight Shooter*, one of their more upbeat numbers.
Spanish Harlem was next. The two songs that received the loudest applause
were *California Dreaming* and *Monday Monday*.

John Phillips then introduced his close friend Scott McKenzie to sing the
song he had written for the then unknown artist. John had written it
specifically for Monterey.

If You're Going to San Francisco — (be sure to wear some flowers in your hair).

The song had been released in early May and by the time he sang it at
Monterey, it was number four on the charts.

The time had come for the finale of the festival when The Mamas & the Papas joined Scott on stage to sing *Dancing in the Streets*. Mama Cass sang the lead vocals, and it was a fitting end to what became known as a legendary pop festival.

All the artists performed free of charge except for Ravi Shankar, who insisted on being paid $3000.

Proceeds benefited two non-profit organisations, the Monterey County Film Commission and the Monterey International Pop Festival Foundation.

The Monterey International Pop Festival Foundation is a non-profit charitable and educational foundation empowering music-related personal development, creativity, and mental and physical health.

Sarah and Mike experienced an event that would never be repeated in their lifetimes, or so they thought. They not only had the opportunity to see some of the best performers in the world, but they also got to meet and talk with some of them.

The young couple waited until Monday afternoon when most of the 90,000 attendees had gone. They returned to NASA to continue their lives in the space age.

During the time of the festival, over 100 Allied soldiers lost their lives in Vietnam.

A GIRL FROM THE
MIDWEST

CHAPTER 17

Margaret Heafield was born in Paoli, Indiana. Her father was a university professor, and her mother was a schoolteacher. Margaret went to school where her parents chose to send her and she travelled on a school bus reserved for whites; in other words, she was a white kid.

Margaret was a dedicated maths and science pupil, and she was intrigued by how things worked. She was a grade A student at Hancock High School and went on to study maths and philosophy at Earlham College in Richmond Indiana.

Her mentor at Earlham was a gifted mathematician named Florence Long. It was she who inspired Margaret's ambition to teach maths. NASA had other ideas for this young woman although she did teach initially.

The preeminent occasion at college was the graduation prom. All the graduating students would dress up in their finest to attend the big night.

Margaret's closest friend, Mary Anne Campbell, approached Margaret after philosophy class.

'Margie, do you want to join me for a soda at the Mint Julep?
'Sure Mary Anne. I would never say no to a caramel ice cream soda.'

The two young women walked the half mile to their favourite soda fountain. They talked the whole way, but not about what Mary Anne really had on her mind.

They ordered their ice cream sodas and sat down in one of the booths with a Selectomatic. The top of the charts was *Heartbreak Hotel* by Elvis Presley, and that's what they chose to play followed by *Don't Be Cruel, My Prayer* by the Platters, and finally *Hound Dog* by Elvis Presley.

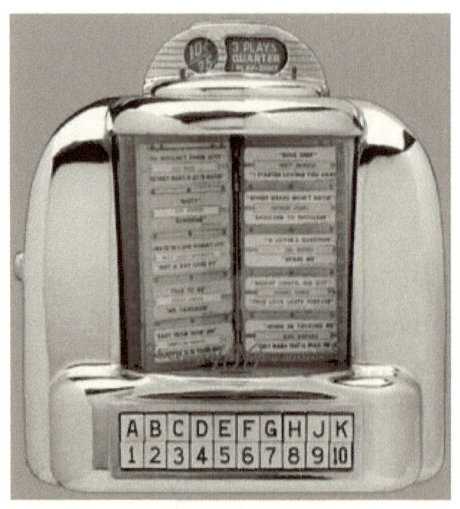

Selectomatic Juke Box

'I've got something very exciting to tell you, Margie,' Mary Anne said.
'You've got a new boyfriend to take you to the prom,' guessed Margaret.
'No, but it does have something to do with the prom.'
'Well, come out with it, girl.'
'You've been voted to be our Homecoming Queen.'
'Don't be ridiculous. I'm not pretty enough to be the Homecoming Queen.'
'It's not all about how pretty you are. It's more on how popular you are with the other students. By the way, you are pretty enough— you're selling yourself short.'
'Well, I'm flabbergasted. What's involved?'
'You will be required to help organise the night alongside the Class President.'
'So I get to work with James Hamilton?'

'You do. Is that a plus?'

'I don't even know him. He's said hello a couple of times.'

The first organising meeting took place in the school library after hours. James introduced himself to Margaret and from that first meeting he decided this was the girl he would marry, which he did in 1959.

Soon after the honeymoon, they moved to Cambridge Massachusetts where James studied law at Harvard University. Margaret gave birth to a daughter, Lauren, soon after.

Margaret was offered a position at the Massachusetts Institute of Technology (MIT) in 1959 as a programmer for the Weather Bureau where she was regarded highly for her skill and accuracy. In 1960 she began writing software for SAGE, an organisation that developed software to find and track enemy aircraft. One of the problems the project encountered was the number of bugs found in the programs. Margaret Hamilton developed software to detect such errors and fix them.

Margaret relished the work and would bring Lauren into the computer lab on weekends. Although very few women worked in computer technology, she was accepted. The mainframe computers she programmed were state of the art.

Mainframe computer 1960

Her work at MIT caught the attention of some key people at the Draper Lab.

The Draper Laboratory is an American not-for-profit research and development organization, headquartered in Cambridge, Massachusetts. Its official name is The Charles Stark Draper Laboratory, Inc.
The Draper Lab was developing software for the Apollo missions and Margaret welcomed the opportunity to help America win the space race. Hamilton continued to excel and by 1965, she was appointed a director of her team.
The critical task for her team was to write software for the Apollo 11's two portable computers. The first of these computers would be located on Apollo 11 and the second would be aboard The Eagle moon lander. Portable in 1965 meant 32 kilograms. Each computer boasted 2K of memory and had 1500 times less processing power than an iPhone

Apollo 11 Portable Computer

The top of the charts in 1965 was *Wooly Bully* by Sam the Sham & the Pharaohs. Sam beat the Beatles, Rolling Stones, Gerry & the Pacemakers and many other top bands to the top place.

FLY ME TO THE MOON

CHAPTER 18

"Wapakoneta" means white cloth in the native Indian language, indicating it was an area of peace. It is a small town in Ohio where nothing much happens, but on August 5, 1930, an event occurred which would place this sleepy village on the world map. Neil Armstrong was born there, and he eventually became the first man to walk on the moon.

Flying had always intrigued Neil, and as a boy he gained his student pilot's licence at the age of 16. He began his tertiary studies in aeronautical engineering compliments of a Navy scholarship and trained as a pilot in the

Navy as part of his course. He served in the Korean War, flying 78 missions without mishap. On his return, he joined NACA, the precursor to NASA, serving as a test pilot as well as utilising his engineering skills.

He admitted his greatest, yet scariest, flight was flying the X-15, which could reach a top speed of 4,000 miles per hour.

X 15 Rocket Plane

Neil met and married his wife Janet Shearon in January 1956, the year before Sputnik was launched. Their first-born Eric arrived in 1957 followed soon after by a girl, Karen. Tragedy struck when Karen died of a brain tumour in 1962. Their third child, Mark, was born the following year— the same year Armstrong joined the astronaut program. The family moved to Houston, Texas, and soon after Neil flew as command pilot on his first mission in Gemini VIII.

Launch of Gemini 8

Once in orbit he and his fellow astronaut, David Scott, managed to dock with another vehicle, Agena... the first time this had been achieved in a manned space flight. The Soviets had achieved a docking by two unmanned space vehicles on October 30, 1967.

Gemini VIII was the most complicated mission to date and would require precise manoeuvring by Armstrong.

The procedure went smoothly. Armstrong and Scott performed faultlessly despite it being their first space flight.

The command module radioed back to Huston. *'We have a serious problem here.'*

The thrusters on both Agena and Gemini were firing out of control, spinning the two still connected space ships wildly. Armstrong reacted quickly, undocking Agena and hoping that would stabilise Gemini.

The result was that Gemini began spinning even faster at one revolution per second. Both astronauts began losing their vision and the fear was they would both lose consciousness. Armstrong had retained enough decision-making power to shut down the thrusters completely. This action would ensure they wouldn't spin any faster, but it wouldn't slow them down either.

Again, Armstrong demonstrated his skill and intelligence. He knew the action he was about to take could cost his and his partner's lives, but he felt he had no other choice.

Gemini had backup thrusters, which were used during re-entry. Employing them now would leave them dangerously short of fuel. Knowing he had no alternative he switched to the backup control, which enabled him to manually fire opposite thrusters which he hoped would stop the spin. It did.

Now that the ship was stable they could concentrate on how they could return safely to Earth with only a quarter of the fuel remaining.

Mission Control began to plan for an emergency landing. Instead of splashing down in the Atlantic, as planned, Gemini 8 would have to re-enter the atmosphere beyond the range of NASA's tracking stations, over China, and land 500 miles east of Okinawa.

Armstrong's quick thinking and flying skills impressed the senior management at NASA. They now knew who would be the first man to walk on the moon.

July 16, 1969

Neil Armstrong, Buzz Aldrin and Michael Collins were launched into space on Apollo 11, heading for a rendezvous with the moon.

Serving as the mission's commander, Armstrong piloted the Lunar Module to the moon's surface on July 20, 1969, with Buzz Aldrin aboard. Collins remained in the command module.

At 10:56 pm, Armstrong exited the Lunar Module. He said, "That's one small step for man, one giant leap for mankind," as he made his famous first step on the moon.

For about two and a half hours, Armstrong and Aldrin collected samples and conducted experiments. They also took photographs, including their own footprints.

Returning on July 24, 1969, the Apollo 11 craft came down in the Pacific Ocean west of Hawaii. The USS Hornet picked up the crew and the craft, and the three astronauts were put into quarantine for three weeks.

Before long, the three Apollo 11 astronauts were given a warm welcome home. Crowds lined the streets of New York City to cheer on the famous heroes who were honoured in a ticker tape parade. Armstrong received numerous awards for his efforts, including the Medal of Freedom and the Congressional Space Medal of Honour.

Apollo Crew Ticker Tape Parade NYC

Something else of significance occurred in 1969; something which would become just as famous as the moon landing.

WOODSTOCK

CHAPTER 19

By the time we got to Woodstock
We were half a million strong
And everywhere there was song and celebration
And I dreamed I saw the bombers
Riding shotgun in the sky
And they were turning into butterflies
Above our nation

Joni Mitchell

New York City January 1969

Michael Lang and Arthur Kornfeld were drinking coffee in their favourite coffee shop, Abraco's, on 7th Street Manhattan. The two young men were involved in the music industry. Michael was a promoter, producer and manager while Arthur, albeit a musician, was also a record producer and record executive.

Michael had organised the Miami Pop Festival in 1968. It attracted 25,000 people and was headlined by Jimmie Hendrix. It was regarded as a great success.

Little Collins Café

New York

Two business partners were dining in their favourite café. Little Collins was owned by two Australians and named after a well-known café street in Melbourne.

'I'm happy with the progress of Media Sound. I predict it's going to become the preeminent recording studio on the east coast,' said Joel Roseman.

'I think you're right, buddy. It's got everything going for it,' said John Roberts.
Early in 1969, Roberts and Rosenman were New York City entrepreneurs, in the process of building Media Sound, a large audio recording studio complex in Manhattan.

'What do you think about this proposal to develop a smaller studio at Woodstock?'

'To be honest, I'm not sure. Apart from Bob Dylan and the Band, who else would it attract?' asked Joel.

'Have you heard of these guys who are proposing it?'

'I've heard of Lang. He promoted the Miami Pop Festival.'

'Maybe we should meet them. They sound full on. You never know; they may have another proposal we could look at funding.'

'Why don't we ask Miles Lourie to set up a meeting? After all he passed on the proposal to us. Is he acting for them as well?'

'I'm not sure. I wouldn't be surprised. He's a good lawyer.'

Joel contacted Lourie and asked him to set up a meeting with Lang and Kornfeld for the following week. They met at Little Collins for lunch.

Once the introductions and small chat were completed, Roberts broached the subject of the Studio in the Woods.

'Guys, we have considered your proposal and to be perfectly honest we don't think it's a project for us. However, we both admire your entrepreneurship and enthusiasm and would consider investing in another project. Michael, you created and managed the Miami Pop Festival and by all accounts, it was a great success. Why don't we do the same concept but on a larger scale?'

'Actually, I really enjoyed Miami,' Michael said. 'What do you think, Artie?'

'Let me get this clear. You're proposing we two join with you two to create a company to run a pop festival?'

'That's right. Are you up for it, Artie?' asked John.

'I think it would be great! Let's do it.'

Woodstock Ventures was formed, and they rented offices at 47 West 57th Street, Manhattan.

With four very different partners, differences of opinion were bound to happen. Roberts was the disciplined one. He knew what was needed to make the venture succeed. Lang was quite the opposite, being lackadaisical regarding finances. Roberts and Roseman thought seriously about pulling out, but they persevered.

To make the festival work they needed top-line acts. The first group to sign up was Creedence Clearwater Revival for the then princely sum of $10,000.

Prior to CCR signing the boys were finding it difficult to attract big name groups. Once word got around that CCR had signed, many of the top groups followed, although there were many omissions.

Woodstock Ventures was, as the name implied, formed to make a profit, so tickets for the three-day festival cost $42. Ticket sales were restricted to record stores in the greater New York area or by mail order. Approximately 186,000 tickets were sold. The venture anticipated 200,000 festivalgoers would turn up.

John Roberts, Joel Roseman, Artie Kornfeld, Michael Lang

Lang took off to look for a suitable site, but he returned two weeks later empty-handed. Frustrated, Roberts and Rosenman went looking and eventually discovered a suitable venue; the 300-acre Mills Industrial Park in the town of Wallkill, New York, which Woodstock Ventures leased for $10,000 in the spring of 1969. Town officials were assured that no more than 50,000 would attend. Town residents immediately opposed the project. In early July, the Town Board passed a law requiring a permit for any gathering over 5,000 people. On July 15, 1969, the Wallkill Zoning Board of Appeals officially banned the concert on the basis that the planned portable toilets would not meet town code. Reports of the ban, however, turned out to be a publicity bonanza for the festival with widespread media reports across the country.

The Woodstock group, now desperate to find a suitable venue, were introduced to a local dairy farmer named Sam Yasgur.

Commercial Centre on Yasgur's Farm

Yasgur's land formed a natural bowl sloping down to Filippini Pond on the land's north side. The stage would be set up at the bottom of the hill with Filippini Pond forming a backdrop.

The organisers told Bethel authorities they expected no more than 50,000 people.

Despite resident opposition, Bethel Town Attorney Frederick W. V. Schadt and building inspector Donald Clark approved the permits, but the Bethel Town Board refused to issue them formally. Clark was ordered to post stop-work orders.

The late change in venue did not give the festival organisers enough time to prepare. At a meeting three days before the event, organisers felt they had two options: one was to complete the fencing and ticket booths, without which the promoters would lose any potential profit. The other option involved putting their available resources into building the stage, without which the promoters feared they would have a disappointed and disgruntled audience and acts. When the audience began arriving by the tens of thousands the next day, the Wednesday before the weekend, the decision was made for them. Those without tickets simply walked through gaps in the fences, and the organisers were forced to make the event free of charge. Though the festival initially left its promoters nearly bankrupt, their ownership of the film and recording rights more than compensated for the losses after the release of the best-selling film in 1970.

After all the trials and tribulations the festival began. The program looked like this:

Friday, August 15 – Saturday, August 16

Artist	Time	Notes
Richie Havens	5:07 pm – 7:00 pm	Was moved up to the opening performance slot after police stopped Sweetwater en route to the festival and other artists were delayed on the freeway.
Swami Satchidananda	7:10 pm – 7:20 pm	Gave the opening speech/invocation for the festival.
Sweetwater	7:30 pm – 8:10 pm	
Bert Sommer	8:20 pm – 9:15 pm	
Tim Hardin	9:20 pm – 9:45 pm	
Ravi Shankar	10:00 pm – 10:35 pm	Played through the rain.

Melanie	10:50 pm – 11:20 pm	Sent onstage for an unscheduled performance after the Incredible String Band declined to perform during the rainstorm.
Arlo Guthrie	11:55 pm – 12:25 am	
Joan Baez	12:55 am – 2:00 am	Was six months pregnant at the time.

Saturday, August 16 – Sunday, August 17

Artist	Time	Notes
Quill	12:15 pm – 12:45 pm	
Country Joe McDonald	1:00 pm – 1:30 pm	Brought in for an unscheduled emergency solo performance when Santana were not yet ready to take the stage. Joe performed again with The Fish the following day.
Santana	2:00 pm – 2:45 pm	Aged 20, Michael Shrieve, the band's drummer, was the youngest musician to play at the festival
John Sebastian	3:30 pm – 3:55 pm	Sebastian was not on the bill, but rather was attending the festival, and was

		recruited to perform while the promoters waited for many of the scheduled performers to arrive.
Keef Hartley Band	4:45 pm – 5:30 pm	
The Incredible String Band	6:00 pm – 6:30 pm	Originally slated to perform on the first day following Ravi Shankar; declined to perform during the rainstorm and were moved to the second day.
Canned Heat	7:30 pm – 8:30 pm	
Mountain	9:00 pm – 10:00 pm	
Grateful Dead	10:30 pm – 12:05 am	Their set was cut short after the stage amps overloaded during *Turn on Your Love Light*.
Creedence Clearwater Revival	12:30 am – 1:20 am	
Janis Joplin with The Kozmic Blues Band	2:00 am – 3:00 am	
Sly and the Family Stone	3:30 am – 4:20 am	

The Who	5:00 am – 6:05 am	Briefly interrupted by Abbie Hoffman
Jefferson Airplane	8:00 am – 9:40 am	Joined onstage on piano by Nicky Hopkins.

Sunday, August 17 – Monday, August 18

Artist	Time	Notes
Joe Cocker and The Grease Band	2:00 pm – 3:25 pm	Played *With a Little Help from My Friends*. After Joe Cocker's set, a thunderstorm disrupted the events for several hours.
Country Joe and the Fish	6:30 pm – 8:00 pm	Country Joe McDonald's second performance.
Ten Years After	8:15 pm – 9:15 pm	
The Band	10:00 pm – 10:50 pm	
Johnny Winter	12:00 am – 1:05 am	Winter's brother, Edgar Winter, is featured on three songs.
Blood, Sweat & Tears	1:30 am –	

	2:30 am	
Crosby, Stills, Nash & Young	3:00 am – 4:00 am	An acoustic and electric set was played. Neil Young skipped most of the acoustic set.
Paul Butterfield Blues Band	6:00 am – 6:45 am	
Sha Na Na	7:30 am – 8:00 am	
Jimi Hendrix / Gypsy Sun & Rainbows	9:00 am – 11:10 am	Performed to a considerably smaller crowd of fewer than 200,000 people.

Many acts were invited but declined for various reasons including:

Bob Dylan

Simon and Garfunkel

The Jeff Beck Group

Led Zeppelin

The Byrds

Chicago

The Moody Blues

Frank Zappa

The Doors

Joni Mitchell

Jethro Tull

500,000 well-behaved music lovers turned up to Woodstock. It is best depicted in the following images.

Only two deaths occurred. One was an overdose, and the other was run over by a tractor while he was sleeping. Two births occurred.

By the time we got to Woodstock

Stage

Joe Cocker

Jimmie Hendrix

Janis Joplin

The Crowd

Skinny Dipping

NAPALM IN THE MORNING

CHAPTER 20

1962

Melbourne

McKittrick Road Bentleigh was like many other quiet tree-lined streets in Bentleigh. The area was abundant with baby boomers. Many of these kids' parents were making their mark as successful employees or self-employed business people. The 60s were a time of a booming economy. The world was experiencing significant post-war growth.

I lived at number 8, McKittrick Road. Next door was Geoff Bennet. Opposite were Noel Parsons and Paul Fagan.

We played many street games such as cricket and football. The most popular game was war.

The game of war required machine guns. These were difficult to come by. We, therefore, fashioned our own out of timber found in our fathers' work sheds. My gun was rudimentary as were Geoff's and Paul's. Noel was very clever with his hands and his gun had a telescopic sight with copper wire crosshairs.

The game was not restricted to the street. All four front and backyards were part of the battlefield.

The belligerents were Australia versus either Japan or Germany. Australia did not always win.

By the time we all reached thirteen, we were more interested in girls than war.

While my friends and I were playing World War 2 in 1962, Robert Menzies sent 30 military advisers to Vietnam.

That decision would shape Australia's future.

My life continued through the sixties. I entered university in 1969; a significant year when Neil Armstrong and Buzz Aldrin walked on the moon. I lost my virginity to a sweet girl called Terry.

By this time the Vietnam War was at its height. The student body and many others in the community were protesting our involvement. I marched in the Melbourne Moratorium against the war.

A Brief History of the Vietnam War

The Vietnam War began in the 1950s though the conflict in Southeast Asia had its roots in the French colonial period of the 1800s. The United States, Australia, New Zealand, France, China, the Soviet Union, Cambodia, Laos and other countries would, over time, become involved in the lengthy war. Finally, it ended in 1975 when North and South Vietnam were reunited as one country.

Vive La France

1887

Napoleon III imposes a colonial system encompassing Vietnam and later Cambodia and Laos.

1923-1925

A young Vietnamese nationalist called Ho Chi Minh is invited by the Soviet Union to travel to Moscow and train as an agent of Comitern (Communist International)

February 1930

Ho Chi Minh founds the Indochinese Communist Party.

September 1940

Japanese troops invade French Indochina, occupying Vietnam. The French offer very little resistance.

Invading Japanese Forces

May 1941

Ho Chi Minh establishes the League for the Independence of Vietnam, commonly known as the Viet Minh. Its purpose is to resist the French and Japanese occupation of Vietnam.

March 1945

The Japanese orchestrate a coup expelling the French and declaring Vietnam, Laos and Cambodia independent countries.

August 1945

Japan surrenders to the Allies leaving Indochina in a precarious position.

France once more exerts its authority over Vietnam.

September 1945

Ho Chi Minh establishes an independent North Vietnam.

July 1946

The French government offers Ho Chi Minh limited self-government. The offer is rejected. The guerrilla war against the French begins.

June 1949

Bao Dai, the last emperor of Vietnam, is appointed Vietnam's head of state by the French.

January 1950

China and the Soviet Union recognise the Democratic Republic of Vietnam. Both countries begin supplying their communist ally with military and economic aid to support the resistance fighters. The Viet Minh ramp up their attacks against the French.

June 1950

The USA identifies the Viet Minh as a Communist threat. They provide assistance to France to combat the Communist insurgents.

March-May 1954

The French are soundly defeated at Dien Bien Phu, bringing about the end of French rule in Indochina.

April 1954

The US president Dwight D Eisenhower in a speech uses the term "domino theory" in relation to Southeast Asia.

July 1954

The Geneva Accords establishes North and South Vietnam divided at the 17th parallel. The accords also stipulate that elections will be held within two years to unify the country under a single democratic government. Elections are never held.

The South is led by a Catholic nationalist, Ngo Dinh Diem while the North continues to be led by Ho Chi Minh.

May 1959

North Vietnamese build a supply route from the north into the south known as the Ho Chi Minh trail.

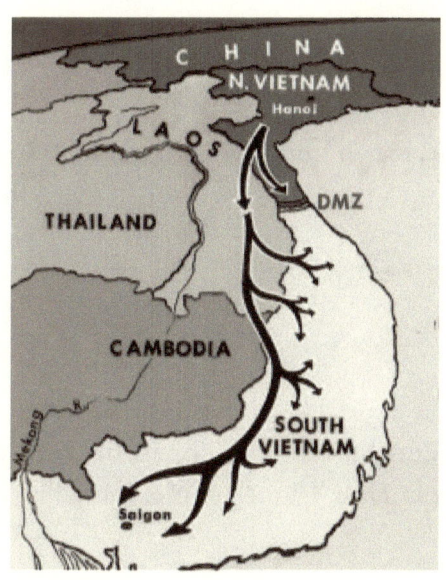

July 1959

A raid on U.S. soldiers' living quarters near Saigon leaves several dead. These are the first American casualties of war

September 1960

Due to his ill health, Ho Chi Minh is replaced by Le Duan.

May 1961

President Kennedy dispatches 400 soldiers supported by helicopters to support the South Vietnamese war effort.

February 1962

Ngo Dinh Diem survives a bomb blast targeting the presidential palace. His nepotism to the Catholic minority was the motivation for the assailants.

May 1963

Ngo Dinh Diem orders his troops to open fire on a gathering of Buddhist protesters in Hue. Eight people, including children, are killed.

June 1963

A Buddhist monk immolates himself at a busy intersection, creating worldwide news coverage.

November 1963

The U.S. government realises Diem must go. They back a military coup to expel him. He is brutally killed along with his brother.

August 1964

North Vietnamese patrol boats in the Gulf of Tonkin attack the USS Maddox. President Johnson authorises air strikes on several North Vietnamese patrol boat bases. Two aircraft are shot down and Everett Alvarez Jr. becomes the first POW captured by the North. He remains their guest for over eight years.

Everett Alvarez Jr.

Congress passes the Gulf of Tonkin Resolution authorising the president to take "all necessary measures including the use of armed force" against any aggressor.

November 1964

The Soviets boost military support to North Korea, dispatching aircraft, artillery, small arms, radar, defence systems, food and medical supplies. The Chinese send engineers to establish the North's defence infrastructure.

February 1965

President Johnson orders the bombing of strategic targets in North Vietnam in retaliation of Viet Cong raids on American targets.

Soon after, Johnson launches a three-year bombing campaign of targets in North Vietnam and the Ho Chi Minh Trail. The operation is named "Rolling Thunder". In March 1965, U.S. Marines land on beaches near Da Nang, South Vietnam. These are the first U.S. boots on the ground in Vietnam in significant numbers.

July 1965

President Johnson orders 50,000 additional ground troops to be sent to Vietnam.

The draft is now 35,000 a month.

November 1965

Protests against the war are becoming more prolific; Norman Morrison, a 31-year-old pacifist, sets himself alight in front of the Pentagon in protest against the war.

THE SUN FINAL

Baltimore Quaker With Baby Sets Self Afire, Dies In War Protest At Pentagon
Lindsay Beats Beame In New York Mayoral Race

November 1965

In the first large scale battle known as the Battle of la Drang Valley, three hundred American troops are killed. In what will become the American Modus Operandi, troops are both dropped in and withdrawn by helicopter.

U.S. troop numbers in Vietnam rise to 400,000.

June 1966

For the first time, American bombers hit Hanoi and Haiphong.

U.S. troop numbers stationed in Vietnam increase to 500,000.

August 18, 1966

The Battle of Long Tan

The Battle of Long Tan in a rubber plantation in South Vietnam in 1966 could have been an Australian military disaster but is instead remembered as a decisive victory.

On August 18, 1966, D Company 6 RAR Battalion, consisting of 105 Australians, along with a three-man New Zealand artillery team, entered the Long Tan rubber plantations.

They had taken over from B Company in pursuit of enemy forces which a day earlier had attacked the Australian operations base at Nui Dat in Phuoc Tuy province.

About 3.30pm, a group of Viet Cong walked into the middle of the patrolling Australian soldiers who opened fire, wounding one and forcing the others to flee.

The Australian soldiers continued their advance, the three platoons of D Company - designated 10, 11 and 12 - taking up positions around the rubber plantation.

Just after 4.00pm, the 28 men of 11 Platoon came under heavy fire from multiple directions, killing several soldiers and pinning them down.

As torrential rain began to pour, artillery support was called in from Nui Dat as it became clear the Australians were facing forces better equipped and more numerous than expected.

Later intelligence showed they were facing a combined force of the Viet Cong 275th Regiment and the local D445 Provincial Mobile Battalion - between 1,500 and 2,500 soldiers.

10 Platoon attempted to rendezvous with their trapped colleagues - intercepting and killing a group of attackers before they too were attacked on three sides and their radio destroyed.

A radio operator braved enemy fire to restore communications and 10 Platoon was ordered to withdraw under cover of artillery fire.

Meanwhile, Vietnamese forces had advanced on 11 Platoon in a bid to negate the artillery support.

Artillery was walked closer to the pinned down troops, with shells falling less than 100 metres from the Australians.

Two 9 Squadron RAAF helicopters were called in to resupply the platoon, and were forced to fly through torrential rain, with visibility close to zero, to drop crates of ammunition.

A resupplied 11 Platoon moved to withdraw, meeting up with parts of 12 Platoon who were engaged nearby and eventually reforming with the rest of D Company.

The Australian forces were deployed in a defensive position as the enemy closed in, launching human wave assaults of infantry across the rubber plantation.

After several hours of intense fighting, reinforcements from B Company arrived on foot, along with A Company on board armoured personnel carriers dispatched from Nui Dat.

Three-and-a-half hours after the battle had started, the Vietnamese disengaged, and the fighting stopped as quickly as it had begun.

Over the next two days, clean-up operations were carried out on the battlefield, rescuing the wounded and recovering the bodies of those killed.

Eighteen Australians were killed - 17 from D Company and one from the 1st Armoured Personnel Carrier Squadron. Twenty-one were wounded.

Two hundred and forty-five Vietnamese dead were found on the battlefield, with captured documents later suggesting hundreds more had been killed or wounded.

The Australian soldiers had been outnumbered 20 to 1 and despite their success against overwhelming odds, the Battle of Long Tan was still the costliest battle for Australia during the entire Vietnam War.

ABC News Report

April 1967

The protest movement was becoming stronger around the world.

Protest San Francisco

Protests in Australia were just as vigilant.

Protest in Melbourne Australia

London Protest March

September 1967

Nguyen Van Thieu wins the presidential election.

January 1968

The Tet Offensive begins, comprising a combined assault of Viet Minh and North Vietnamese armies. Attacks are carried out in more than 100 cities and outposts across South Vietnam, including Hue and Saigon, and the U.S. Embassy is invaded. The effective, bloody attacks shock U.S. officials and mark a turning point in the war and the beginning of a gradual U.S. withdrawal from the region.

February 11 – 17 1968

The worst week in the war for the Americans with 543 killed in battle.

February – March 1968

Battles of Hue and Saigon clear the Viet Cong from both cities.

March 16, 1968

The Mai Lai massacre with more than 500 civilians murdered by U.S. forces.

March 1968

President Johnson halts bombing in North Vietnam north of the 20th parallel. He announces he will not be seeking re-election.

November 1968

Richard Nixon is elected on a promise to end the draft.

September 1969

Ho Chi Minh dies of a heart attack in Hanoi.

December 1969

The U.S. government introduces the draft lottery despite Nixon's election promise.

1969-1972

Nixon gradually reduces the number of U.S. forces in Vietnam. The South Vietnamese are required to take more responsibility.

From a peak of 540,000 in 1969, there were 69,000 troops in 1972.

February 1970

Henry Kissinger begins secret peace negotiations with Le Duc Tho of the North Vietnamese government.

March 1969 – May 1970

The U.S. bomb neutral Cambodia, knowing the military action is illegal.

June 1970

Congress repeals the Gulf of Tonkin Resolution to control the president's ability to use force at his discretion.

January 1971

American and South Vietnamese forces invade Laos in an attempt to cut the Ho Chi Minh trail. The operation fails.

June 1971

The New York Times publishes the Pentagon Papers, revealing the U.S. government has secretly increased involvement in the war.

December 1972

Richard Nixon authorises the most intensive air attack of the war in Operation Linebacker. The air attacks drop 20,000 tons of bombs over densely populated regions.

January 22, 1973

Former President Johnson dies in Texas at age 64.

The Selective Service announces the end to the draft and institutes an all-volunteer military.

January 27, 1973

President Nixon signs the Paris Peace Accords, ceasing U.S. involvement in the Vietnam War.

February – April 1973

North Vietnam returns 591 American prisoners of war in what is known as Operation Homecoming. John McCain is one of those released.

August 1974

President Nixon resigns in the face of likely impeachment after the Watergate Scandal is revealed. Gerald R. Ford becomes president.

January 1975

President Ford rules out any further U.S. military involvement in Vietnam.

April 1975

Saigon falls to Communist forces and the South Vietnam government surrenders. Helicopters transport over 1000 American civilians and 7000 South Vietnamese in a mass evacuation.

Evacuating Saigon

July 1975

Unification of North and South under communist rule becomes a reality.

By the end of the war, more than 58,000 Americans and 521 Australians lost their lives. Other countries that fought alongside the Americans and South Vietnamese were South Korea, with 5000 killed, New Zealand, with 37 killed and Canada, with 100 killed. Vietnam would later release estimates that 1.1 million North Vietnamese and Viet Cong fighters were killed, up to 250,000 South Vietnamese soldiers died and more than 2 million civilians were killed on both sides of the war.

2019

Vietnam is now a popular holiday destination.

FRENCH REVOLUTION

THE OTHER ONE

CHAPTER 21

May 1967

Paris

The University of Paris placed a ban on male and female students making dormitory visits. This rule effectively placed a ban on student sex.

Students were more than unhappy about this ruling and staged protests.

January 1968

A new swimming complex was being dedicated at the university. A student leader named Daniel Cohn-Bendit verbally attacked the Minister of Youth and Sports, Francois Missoffe, complaining of the sexual restrictions placed on the student body.

'Why don't you jump in the pool? It may temper your lust,' replied the Minister.

'That's the reply I would expect from a minister of a fascist regime.'

The exchange earned Cohn-Bendit a reputation as an antiauthoritarian provocateur. He soon acquired an almost cult-like following among French youth.

March 1968

Students attacked the offices of American Express, protesting the Vietnam War. Several students were arrested and charged. A demonstration was held at the Nanterre Campus in support of the arrested students and more students were arrested, including Cohn-Bendit.

May 2

The Dean of Nanterre closed the campus. The students decided to demonstrate at the Sorbonne in the Latin Quarter.

May 3

The Rector of the Sorbonne requested the police to clear the university's courtyard of the 300 students who had assembled there.

The volatile situation became a massive riot, encompassing not only the students but also many bystanders. Cobblestones were dislodged from the courtyard and hurled at the police. Barricades were assembled and tear gas and beatings resulted.

The rector closed the Sorbonne, an action which enraged the students even more. Another rally was called for May 10 which would demand the Sorbonne to reopen, the release of students and an end to police action in the Latin Quarter.

May 10-11, 1968

The Night of the Barricades

The number of students had escalated to 40,000. The students began their march on the national broadcasting authority but the police blocked their way.

The students began building barricades and removing cobblestones.

The police were given their orders to attack the students at 2am. They rushed the demonstrators, firing tear gas. Their beatings were relentless to both students and bystanders. The police action continued until dawn the next morning. By then, 500 students were arrested with many more hospitalised, including over 250 police officers. The general population sided with the students.

What began as a student protest against dormitory visit restrictions and educational reform engulfed the whole of France.

Social change was demanded, including the democratisation of social and cultural institutions incorporating education and the news media.

The largest wildcat strikes in French history enveloped the entire country, with millions of workers taking to the streets in support of the students as well as their own demands. Many factories were occupied, including the giant French automakers Renault and Citroen.

France survived the crisis although it was badly shaken. President de Gaulle arrived back from Germany where he tried to get the French occupying forces to return to France to quell the riots and strikes.

When he addressed the French people on May 30, he intimated the troubles were instigated by an attempted communist takeover. This was a complete falsehood; in fact, the communists were not supportive of the student movement.

The Grenelle Accords were offered to the workers, whereby they would receive wage increases and better working conditions. The accord was rejected by the workers who continued to strike.

President de Gaulle called for new elections on the grounds that the country yearned for stability. He was right. His government was returned with an increased majority.

Buoyed by his strong win, he announced a national referendum on regional reorganisation and Senate reform. It failed to win the support of the people. General de Gaulle left politics forever.

Cohn-Bendit went on to be a politician representing the Greens. He was elected to the European Parliament in 1994.

A DECADE TO REMEMBER

CHAPTER 22

The sixties were a decade of extremes. It began with hope when mankind first began exploring space. The threat of a nuclear holocaust soon followed. A young president who promised so much was cut down in his prime. The Beatles and Rolling Stones changed the music scene forever. More bombs were dropped on North Vietnam than in World War Two in its entirety.

In America, Civil Rights were achieved but at what cost.

I was eight in 1960 and eighteen in 1969. I remember so much of the experience; some of it was exciting and exhilarating. Some of it was frightening, and some of it was sad. It all ended sitting around a 21-inch TV with friends watching Armstrong and Aldrin walk on the moon.

The sixties was like no other decade before or since.

The End

BIBLIOGRAPHY

W   Margaret Hamilton (scientist) - Wikipedia

W   Katherine Johnson - Wikipedia

W   Sputnik 1 - Wikipedia

G   explorer 1 satellite - Google Search

   Explorer 1 Overview | NASA

a   Margaret and the Moon: Dean Robbins, Lucy Knisley: 9780399551857: Amazon.com: Books

S   The Space Race Begins | NASA: Challenging the Space Frontier | Scholastic.com

W   Sputnik 1 - Wikipedia

F   Sixty Years Later, Sputnik Declassifications Offer Primer in Fake News

   The secrets of the Space Race

W   Timeline of the Space Race - Wikipedia

   V1 and V2 Rockets - Engineering and Technology History Wiki

   The Rest of the Rocket Scientists | Page 2 | Space | Air & Space Magazine

G   a simple description of allies taking Belin - Google Search

   WERNHER von BRAUN: SURRENDER TO THE AMERICANS

Neil Armstrong · Life, Children & Moon Landing · Biography

List of performances and events at Woodstock Festival · Wikipedia

Woodstock · Wikipedia

Rosa Parks · Life, Bus Boycott & Death · Biography

Berlin Wall built · HISTORY

Martin Luther King Jr. · Wikipedia

Timeline: Martin Luther King, Jr. · Part IV

Vietnam War Timeline · HISTORY

SparkNotes: The Vietnam War (1945–1975): Brief Overview

May 1968 events in France · Wikipedia

May 1968: A Month of Revolution Pushed France Into the Modern World · The New York Times

events of May 1968 | Background, Significance, & Facts | Britannica.com

Daniel Cohn-Bendit Facts

hippie | History, Lifestyle, & Beliefs | Britannica.com

Bay of Pigs Invasion · Wikipedia

Bay of Pigs Invasion · HISTORY

Brigade 2506 · Wikipedia

Bay of Pigs Chronology

True Story: I Was A Hippie In San Francisco In The Sixties | Cracked.com

First published 2021 by Crabtree Pty Ltd

The Fab Sixties is a work of fiction. Any resemblance to real persons, living or dead, is purely coincidental.

ISBN: 978-0-6451166-2-5 (p/b)
ISBN: 978-0-6451166-3-2 (ebook)

www.ingramcontent.com/pod-product-compliance
Lightning Source LLC
Chambersburg PA
CBHW030524020726
47494CB00004B/1221